Hello, Norma Jean

A Flight of Fantasy with Marilyn Monroe

Sue Dolleris

Savant Books
Honolulu, HI, USA
2010

Published in the USA by Savant Books and Publications
2630 Kapiolani Blvd #1601
Honolulu, HI 96826
http://www.savantbooksandpublications.com

Printed in the USA

Edited by Wallace Klein
Cover by Helen Babalis
Front Cover Photo from the trailer for *Some Like It Hot* (in the public domain), colorization courtesy of Maria deVries
Back Cover Photo from the trailer for *Niagara* (in the public domain)
Interior lip print courtesy of Molumen from Open Clipart Library at http://www.openclipart.org/detail/12061 (in the public domain).
Author photo by Portrait Innovations.

13-digit ISBN: 978-0-9845552-6-0
10-digit ISBN: 0-9845552-6-9

Part I of this book is entirely fictional, though it makes reference to non-fictional characters. Part II of this book is non-fictional. Although the author has tried to make the information in this section of the book as accurate as possible, the information comes from many different sources, including numerous websites, and it was not possible to verify the accuracy of every statement included in the book. There may be mistakes, both typographical and in content, and the information conveyed is current only up to the date that the manuscript went into production. Therefore, this text should be used only as a general guide and as an inspiration for further inquiry, not as an authoritative source of information.

No person shall have any right to rely on the information contained in this book, and neither the author, nor the editor, nor the publisher shall be liable or responsible to any person or entity for any injury, loss or damage caused, or alleged to have been caused, directly or indirectly, by the information conveyed in this book.

Dedicated to Nanny for always believing,
and to Bob, Meagan and Erin
for their loving encouragement.

Acknowledgment

I'M THANKFUL

…that I grew up in a home where I was told that as long as I worked hard, I could do and accomplish anything

…for a husband and two daughters who listened to and commented on my countless ideas, many of which never came to fruition (and shouldn't have)

…that I learned to channel inspiration to the page, and finally perfected how to filter that same inspiration (not every idea is a gem)

…for finding patient, professional publisher, Dan Janik, and Savant Books and Publications at just the right time ("build it and they will come" doesn't seem to apply to publishing)

…to Wallace Klein, Savant editor, who dragged me— sometimes kicking and screaming—to a stronger *Hello, Norma Jean* with each painful pass

…to family and close friends who supported my seemingly unreachable goals

…for my stamina, fortitude and high energy that allowed me to always write, write, write, right through a busy schedule of raising a family and working a full-time job

…to Marilyn Monroe, for striking a chord within us all

…and to Norma Jean Baker, for providing the pathway to achieving my number one goal!

Sue Dolleris, 2010

HELLO, NORMA JEAN

PART I

Prologue

Trouble in Paradise

Liberace, glamorous and flamboyant as ever, stands in the middle of the intersection of Paradise Cove and Eden Lane in the northwest sector of Heaven as though commanding center stage in a well-rehearsed musical review. Wearing a glittery aqua jumpsuit and an ermine-lined silver cape, he's surrounded by a dense smoky fog that appears to have just rolled in off the tarmac from the set of *Casablanca*, where Rick is telling Ilsa he is staying behind—but the backdrop here is a brilliant azure cloud-filled sky. This isn't dry-ice fog from a Whitesnake music video; this is the real thing. Wave after wave of curling, hazy smoke rolls in off the billowing clouds.

Liberace is standing behind Gershwin's Chickering baby grand piano. He leans over his demurely-sweatered blonde student's shoulder and, with an exaggerated extension of his arm, reaches past her to tap out the time to the music on the reflection of the elaborate mercury glass candelabra poised on the polished surface of the piano. His student is a pastel haze that appears to fade in and out of the clouds with her ultra light blonde hair and close-fitting cardigan in the palest shade of lavender. She slumps forward over the keyboard, her soft, platinum hair a blur as she fails miserably, once again, in her clumsy attempt to play the piece.

Liberace winces, then gently says, "Again, Marilyn. Try it again."

Marilyn takes a deep breath, sits up straight...and once more slaughters the hauntingly ethereal opening measures of Beethoven's *Moonlight Sonata*. It's virtually unrecognizable except for the familiar first three notes that she has finally mastered. The rest is labored and hesitant, crippled with wrong notes.

With a sweeping motion, Liberace fans his cape—a pose that has been captured for posterity in numerous gilt-framed photos on display next to lavish costumes, candelabra rings and sheet music at the Liberace Museum in Las Vegas. "This time," he insists, "*feel* the music. Only then will Kate be able to hear you." He stops momentarily to listen, then wishes he hadn't. He cringes. "Feel it, don't just plunk at it. Try to really *feel* the music."

Liberace sits next to Marilyn and gently lifts her face to his. Looking up at him is the beautiful and vulnerable face of Marilyn Monroe, her skin porcelain, her lips perpetually pouty. She playfully sticks out her tongue at him. Marilyn removes her hands from the piano keys and shakes them vigorously. "Lee, I never did take direction well."

Liberace laughs. "I know! Billy Wilder told me." Marilyn smiles with feigned exasperation. She looks up at him through lowered lashes, similar to Princess Diana's signature pose. Marilyn pouts. "I always struggled with learning my lines, but at least I had a character to play. It's all I know." Liberace removes his cape and dramatically drapes it across the piano. He then fans his wide jumpsuit collar. There's hard work ahead. "Okay, then play a character who's trying to learn to play the piano. Does that work for you?"

She brightens somewhat, then tries to play again, and again is unsuccessful.

Wilted, Liberace puts his hands on hers to mercifully stop the playing. Then, brightening, he says, "How about this?" In a dramatic deep baritone, like a Coming Attractions announcer, Liberace continues: "FADE IN: EXTERIOR, HEAVEN, CORNER OF PARADISE COVE AND EDEN LANE, ETERNITY."

Excitedly, Marilyn says, "Oh, that's so much better." She tries to play the piece again. This time it's perhaps a slight bit better. Marilyn turns to Liberace. "So did this character take piano lessons before or is this her first time? What's her back story?"

Exasperated, Liberace says, "How about we take a break?" He glances at his three-inch-wide diamond-encrusted watch. "DiMaggio just died and he'll be arriving soon." Liberace stands and stretches like a waking cat. He opens a large door that has appeared in the clearing, and stands aside like the ever-watchful doorman, motioning for her to enter the doorway and beyond. "The Yankee Clipper awaits."

Marilyn straightens. "Time for Joe to arrive?" Liberace answers, "It's March 8, 1999." "I can't believe it!" she says. "Where did the nineties go?" She delicately places her hands in position on the keyboard. "Let me try one more time. Peg over in Admissions will keep Joe busy with paperwork for a while yet."

A man appears in the doorway. The mist clears revealing Beethoven in a crumpled white shirt with a starched high collar and cinched black pinstriped waistcoat and trousers. He looks remarkably like Gary Oldman in *Immortal Beloved*.

Beethoven tilts his head to listen to the melody, his unkempt electrified Don King hairstyle never moving. Sensing that the moment is close, he clutches his chest. His shoulders sway. In a strong Bavarian accent he says, "You're zo cloze, but play from ze heart, dear Marilyn. You must releaze ze muzic." The melodious tones now please Beethoven. He smiles contentedly. Ever so softly, he says, "Vunderbar!"

Liberace pats him on the back. "Beautiful piece, Ludwig. Still holds up to this day."

Beethoven covers his ear at a sour note and shakes his head playfully at Marilyn. She begins again.

Miraculously, the heavens are now filled with beautiful, flowing music.

Beethoven claps. "Congradulayzhunz, Marilyn. You haf now broken down ze vallz."

She beams. "Thank goodness! Kate needs me. I have to reach her."

The haunting melody of Beethoven's *Moonlight Sonata* fills the air.

SUE DOLLERIS

HELLO, NORMA JEAN

"And it seems to me you lived your life
Like a candle in the wind
Never knowing who to cling to
When the rain set in"

From "Candle in the Wind"
Music by Elton John
Lyrics by Bernie Taupin
Written in 1973 in honor of Marilyn Monroe

Chapter One

Facing the Music

It is Saturday, July 31, 1999. Theme park enthusiasts at the sprawling Southern California amusement park gulp $6.00 Dr. Peppers to survive the sweltering heat. Like livestock, they are herded through zigzagging lines toward overcrowded rides, overpriced snacks, and littered restrooms—or the blessed relief of air-conditioned stores selling cheap souvenirs and memorabilia.

In a tiny patch of shade outside Captain Kid's Fish & Chips, Kate Malone Davis and her friend and co-worker, Beth Carter, are sitting with their tanned knees scrunched up to their tanned chests on the undersized benches of an oversized picnic table decked out as a pirate schooner.

During the construction of what would ultimately be Pirate Town in the park's vast expanse, money might have been better spent on more comfortable seating. But Pirate Town is merely a star marked "You are here" in the upper left corner of the $5.00 park map—only one of the million pieces in the amusement park's gigantic puzzle.

Kate, a striking brunette with a cause—she wears a "You Can Do the Can-Can" recycling T-shirt with a full blown can across one breast and a flattened can across the other—passes a wet-nap to Beth, a beauty in coordinated designer casual. The theme for Beth today is turquoise; not the chunky, gauche turquoise jewelry of a Santa Fe photo shoot, rather a watercolor top over a lacy camisole and matching Bermuda length shorts in an ethereal shade that would fall precisely between paint chips poetically named 'Tahitian Sea' and 'Priceless Emerald.'

Kate fluffs her stylish but unkempt shaggy hairstyle while humming the theme from Beethoven's *Moonlight Sonata*, then shakes her head as if to rid herself of the melody. "I can't seem to get that music out of my head."

Beth runs the quick-drying wet-nap across the back of her neck. "Tell me about it. You've been humming it for months now. Been almost nonstop since back at the Tilt-A-Whirl, and that was..." Beth checks her expensive, bronze-tone cuff watch, "three hours ago. Give it a rest already."

These two wilted thrill-seekers, hesitantly waving goodbye to their mid-thirties, pick through the remaining fish nuggets and hush puppies and slurp what's left of their Sno-cones. They're surrounded by elderly visitors shuffling past, leaning on their metal walkers; families who have already checked out of their hotels dragging their luggage-on-wheels; moms pushing baby strollers; and kids in cheap paper pirate hats drooping in the intense heat. Captain Kid's mortified teenage employees wear plastic pirate hoop earrings, bandannas and, adding insult to injury, stuffed cloth parrots pinned to their shoulders.

Kate takes a deep breath and then whispers, "Sure is hot," with a sigh.

Beth folds the disintegrating wet-nap yet again and pours expensive bottled water on it, then lifts her bangs and plasters it to her forehead. "Hot? That's the understatement of the summer. Hot is a sizzling fajita skillet. This is molten lava! And we're in the freakin' shade!" Beth carefully runs a manicured hand under her lower thigh to slowly unstick it from the bench seat. She laments, "Surely this much sun is terrible for the skin. Can't wait to hear what my dermatologist has to say about it during my next scan for moles." Lazily, Beth wet-naps her three-year old daughter's face, then gives the crumpled remnants of the towelette one last swipe across her own forehead. She pulls her shirt away in a fanning motion.

Kate laughs, "What's the matter, Beth? Implants boiling your bazooms?"

Beth straightens slightly. "Could you tell if you didn't know? They're only a full 'C'."

Kate shakes her head, "No, they're very discreet," and adds laughing, "especially since they now sit about four inches from your chin." Kate removes her finger from the end of her straw and lets loose a straw-full of ice water against her wrist. "We could hit the water rides if we weren't stuck over in Kiddie Valley. Where are husbands when you need 'em?"

Beth feigns shock. "You're asking me about husbands?" Beth leans in so the kids won't hear. "I'm practically a virgin again. Just like pierced ears, don't stick anything in there for a long time and they close right up."

Kate stands and starts to clear the mess. "I can't hear you." Kate hums *Moonlight Sonata* as she loads Brady and Blaire, her two-year-old auburn-haired boy/girl twins, into the cumbersome twin stroller.

Beth leans across the table and puts her hand over Kate's mouth to stop the humming. "But I can still hear you," Beth says as she gathers her girls, blonde three-year-old Erin and blonder five-year-old Meagan.

Kate asks, "Brady, do you want any more fish?" Brady's unable to speak because he has a mouthful of hush puppy. He shakes his head no. Before Kate can ask Blaire, she has reached for a fish nugget. "I do, Mommy."

Erin holds up her hands. She runs her fingers against her thumb. "Sticky, Mommy." Beth starts to wipe Erin's hands when Beth's older daughter, Meagan, takes the napkin and finishes the job. Beth pats Meagan's head. "You're Mommy's little helper, Meagan." Meagan smiles proudly.

The ladies start to move out of the area when Beth holds her arm out to stop their progress. "Hold on a minute. The air is actually stirring." They all hold still a brief moment to catch the small hint of a breeze.

No sooner have they resumed their pilgrimage down tree-lined Main Street when Beth notices Erin's untied shoelace. They pull to the side and stop. Kate fans herself with a dog-eared map of the park. "Third shoe-tying of the morning. Shoulda brought a staple gun."

Kate is leaning against a gigantic trashcan that has been painted to look like a chipmunk as a sticky boy approaches. Kate pushes in the trashcan's flap, which serves as the chipmunk's protruding teeth, to enable the boy to throw away the remains of his cotton candy. He gives Kate a sticky, tight-lipped smile, and she suppresses a laugh as she notices that his teeth protrude and look remarkably like those of the chipmunk. A pregnant young woman pushing a stroller with a sleeping one-year old inside waddles over to take his hand. She reminds him firmly, "Tell the nice lady 'thank you,' Jeremiah." The boy can barely form the words since his lips are still stuck together, but he manages to get out "Thwankthu." Kate smiles and replies, "You're very welcome, Jeremiah." As Jeremiah and his mother walk away, Kate and Beth simultaneously hold up crossed fingers. Kate laughs, "Better ward off any airborne pregnancies." Beth counters, "You can never be too safe, although a pregnancy for me would have to be an immaculate conception." Kate sings "Jeremiah was a Bullfrog" in a very deep voice. Beth notes, "You're quite musical today, although I hate to say it, but I actually prefer *Moonlight Sonata*."

Beth spots a family vacating a nearby bench that has been blessed with a patch of shade. She makes a beeline for it, dodging in front of a slow-walking older man dragging a portable oxygen tank. Beth stretches out across the bench to make it clear that she has claimed it. Kate chides her in a hushed voice, "Beth, he needs this more than we do."

Beth begrudgingly sits up to make a portion of the bench available in case the old man needs to sit down to catch his breath. She pats the empty space, "Would you like to sit down?" He stops next to the bench, breathless from dragging his oxygen tank around. "Thanks...but would you ladies...happen to know where..." He stops to catch his breath. "Men's room?"

Kate begins unfolding her map to help him, but Beth just points behind her head. "Back that way about thirty feet. Across from funnel cakes."

"Why, thank you...young lady. You both have...lovely families...beautiful children," then, with a pained look on his face, remembering the purpose of his journey, he manages "Sorry, gotta run," and takes off toward the men's room, dragging his oxygen tank behind him.

"Poor guy," says Kate as the old man retreats. "Makes

my lungs hurt just to hear him gasping like that."

Beth says, "Let's sit for a few minutes, then we'll wander over to Kiddie Land." Kate joins her on the bench. "Let's do. We've walked for eighteen seconds. We can use the rest."

"You know what?" Beth counters. "No sense in both of us being held hostage. You can run over to the water ride and get soaked while I spend a half hour watching the kids ride stationary cars."

Kate can't hide her glee. "Are you sure?"

"Of course," Beth responds, "go ahead. Meagan can push Erin in the stroller while I maneuver the twins."

Kate's up like a shot. She doesn't need to be coaxed. She leans down and kisses her kids. "Mommy will meet you at the Jeep ride. Stay with Beth and be good." Kate slips Meagan a dollar bill. "Thanks for babysitting for me, Meagan." Meagan beams. Kate zips her camera case closed and hands it to Beth. "See you in thirty minutes; surely no more than forty-five."

Minutes later, Kate waits in a long line for the water ride. She's behind a petite lady in her mid-forties who wears a clear vinyl rain poncho over her clothing. The lady turns to Kate, "Can't take any chances." She points to a sign hanging at the turn of the next queuing line, which announces:

FORECAST: SUNNY, FUNNY THEME PARK DAY,
BUT HEAVY SPLASHING AHEAD!
YOU WILL GET WET ON THE ROARIN' RIVER RIDE.

Kate smiles and then fans herself, "I sure hope so. It'll be a welcome relief from this heat." Nine minutes later, a now limp Kate stands first in the snaky line, humming *Moonlight*

Sonata.

The Roarin' River ride is a model of efficiency. A giant raft arrives precisely fifteen seconds after its predecessor's departure. Its eight inhabitants, four of whom are sopping wet, disembark to the left. Almost immediately, Kate, the oldest of her group by about twenty years, and seven others enter the now empty carrier from the right.

Kate excitedly chooses a seat on the left side of the raft that's drenched from the previous ride. "Bound to be a good sign, right...that I'll get soaked?" she asks no one in particular. A preteen boy with buzzed reddish hair sits directly across from Kate and fixes his puberty-bound stare first on her bare legs, then on her chest. He points at her and says with a smirk, "Yeah, a good sign for a wet T-shirt contest." She rebuffs his lewd comment—"Sure, Red, like you would know"—and turns her attention to the rock wall architecture surrounding them.

The ride follows a winding path, slowly at first, then building up speed. It runs the rapids with great force, over scores of huge dips, bumps, and rises, with a stomach-churning non-stop rocking. Roaring music from the soundtrack of *Apocalypse Now*, in particular Wagner's booming and stirring "Ride of the Valkyries," is piped in to accompany each wave. The music swells with the waves. Each bounce is accompanied by a resonant base from the soundtrack. A young boy sings along, very loudly, "Duh, duh, duh, da, da." Another young boy joins in to complete the refrain, "Duh, duh, duh, da." Giant waves splash the raft. A girl of about ten with a face full of freckles gets splashed and laughs goodheartedly, turning her head quickly and spraying her neighbor with jets of water from her wet ponytail.

The raft enters a pitch-dark tunnel. This is the most highly anticipated thrill of the ride. All the kids gasp and scream. Amid the shouts of excitement and laughter, Kate hears a sharp cry for help, followed by a desperate choking sound. She quickly removes her seat belt restraint and stands, trying to keep her balance while groping her way forward in total darkness toward the sound.

The raft rounds a bend in the tunnel, banging against the left wall as it makes the turn. As light from the end of the tunnel begins to make things visible again, Red sees Kate standing, half-crouched, with her arms stretched forward. He yells, "Lady, sit down or they'll stop the ride!" Kate lunges toward Red, shouting, "Get out of my way!" Red, who has no idea what's going on, is shocked into silence. The boy next to Red, who is about nine, with close-cropped hair and a face quickly turning purple, is choking. He is thrashing about, pointing frantically at his throat. The raft is nearing the tunnel's end. Kate pushes Red toward one side and manages to wedge herself in halfway between him and the choking boy. She turns the boy around far enough to try an awkward Heimlich maneuver—awkward, but thankfully sufficient. A big chunk of hard candy flies out of the boy's mouth. His passageway is cleared. He takes a deep gasping breath, followed by a fit of coughing. The young passengers clap and cheer.

At a remote little tree house stationed high up on stilts, discreetly camouflaged in the trees over the Roarin' River ride, a teenage boy with a headset over his unruly hair, wearing a happy face nametag that says "I'm Justin. Can I help you?" eats Cheetos as he monitors the water ride.

An alarm buzzes. Justin taps the monitor screen with an orange finger and then his face quickly turns white as he screams into his headset, "A lady's standing in raft four! Yes, standing!" Taking direction from someone on the other end of his headset who's likely in an air-conditioned office on the other side of the park, Justin repeatedly taps the now-greasy monitor. The buzzing alarm stops. Justin listens a moment for further direction. "Okay, I'll get the raft out of the tunnel first and then stop it until she gets back in her seat." There's a slight pause as Justin checks the monitor. "Yeah, I know that raft number five is fifteen seconds behind. I'll divert it to the other side of the tunnel."

As the raft inches out of the tunnel, much slower than usual, and much too close to the side wall, Kate fumbles awkwardly back to her seat.

In his tree house perch, Justin frantically pushes buttons on the screen in front of him. He watches the screen in horror as the raft stops abruptly, then bounces hard against the rocky wall surface.

Kate can no longer keep her balance; she sails off the raft into the swirling water. Underwater, Kate bumps repeatedly against the still-rocking raft and the rocky wall. She tries to get to the surface to gasp for air, but the heavy raft and the swell keep her under.

In the treetops, Justin leans into his monitor. He sees Kate's abandoned carrier rocking in place as her fellow passengers lean over the side where she has just disappeared. He leans the other way and whispers to himself, "Don't all lean at once or you'll tip the raft," as though trying to will the passengers back from the edge. Justin watches Red being cheered on by the other passengers as he kneels on a seat and leans over, trying to get a better look. Kate's empty seat gets splashed.

Justin is stunned but he acts quickly. He shouts into his headset, "Help! I've stopped the ride but send help to four right away just outside the tunnel! We've got a lady in the drink!" He drops his head into his hands. "There goes my promotion to costumed mascot. Guess I'll be going back to handing out tickets for Skee Ball." Justin peels off his nametag and crumples it.

Beth shifts position on Kiddie Land's hard unyielding slatted bench. She repeatedly checks her watch. Erin and Meagan hang on her. She tries moving them away, but they're too limp to sit upright. Blaire and Brady ride on kiddie motorcycles around an endless track in front of her. They are sweaty and tired, with strands of matted auburn hair sticking to their faces. Beth pushes her girls off her again as Erin whines, "Tired, Mommy." Beth answers distractedly, "I know, honey. Me, too. We'll be going as soon as Kate comes back." Under her breath she adds, "If she comes back."

Now waiting at the exit line for the water raft ride, Beth stands behind Blaire and Brady, who are slumped in the twin stroller. Meagan pushes Erin's stroller back and forth in place. They wait and watch as four dry and four soaked passengers make their way down the winding path toward them. Two men pass, followed by two kids, then three women and a teenage girl. There's no Kate. The group passes by in a wet blur of giddy laughter and wild replays of the ride. Beth leans to look behind the last girl. Still no Kate. Within moments, another eight happy passengers pass by Beth. Kate is not among them.

In the neon-painted and kid-friendly decorated Welcome Center, Beth tries to manage all four tired, whiny kids, while not letting on that she's actually very worried about Kate.

Brandon, a sweet-faced young man of about eighteen, pulls Beth gently aside and speaks in a low funeral manager's voice. "Ma'am, I'm Brandon, Senior Hospitality Agent, and I'm afraid there's been an accident..."

HELLO, NORMA JEAN

Chapter Two

STAT

In the bright hospital room, a young nurse moves quietly but efficiently around her patient. Wearing printed scrubs featuring teddy bears and alphabet letters more appropriate to the Pediatric Ward, she checks Kate's IV and the blinking monitors, then walks toward the door and scrawls some indecipherable numbers on a white board mounted on the wall to one side of the door. She returns to the bed, picks up Kate's hand, and closely inspects Kate's fingernails. They are unnaturally dark. The nurse frowns, then springs into action, leans over Kate and grabs the call button. "Get Doctor Miller, STAT! Possible respiratory distress."

The nurse walks quickly to the door, opens it wide, and stands in the doorway to peer anxiously down the hall. Behind her, a faint glowing shape rises from Kate's pale and lifeless body on the bed. It is draped in translucent white gauze and has Kate's face. The spirit hovers for a moment over the body, then darts to the overhead light just as the nurse, increasingly concerned about the fate of her patient, turns back to glance at the body on the bed. From her perch on the light fixture, the spirit watches the nurse look back and forth a couple of times between the body and the hallway and then impatiently resume her vigil at the door for Doctor Miller and the crash cart.

The spirit makes a nosedive toward the nurse and stops within inches of her right shoulder. It then darts around the room, soars back up to the ceiling light fixture, and finally pauses in its aerobatics to watch Kate herself lying still on the bed below.

The nurse stands aside as a dark-haired female doctor races into the room pushing a waist-high, lipstick red crash cart that looks like a tool chest loaded with Sears Craftsman tools. The nurse closes the door behind her and hurries over to the bed to assist.

Spirit Kate floats softly down to the windowsill and takes a seat next to a collection of McDonald's Teenie Beanie Babies from 1997, the year the twins were born. She watches with interest the preparations going on over her body. As the doctor reaches for the paddles of the defibrillator, she moves suddenly and with great force toward the closed door. Without slowing down or hesitating, Kate's spirit passes effortlessly through the door and into the hospital corridor, where she floats up to glide along the ceiling tiles.

Kate drifts down the hallway and enters a nearby waiting room. She inspects the four–year-old magazines, trashy tabloids, and small TV playing Louie Anderson's revival of *Family Feud*. There are remnants of vending machine candy bars and peanut butter crackers strewn about on the cheap wooden tables. And, of course, there are assorted stricken family members waiting for news of their loved ones from the hospital staff.

The spirit darts to the corner of the small room and hovers over Ray, Kate's husband. He's a tall, thin but muscular man in his late-thirties with close-cropped receding hair. Ray looks pale and totally exhausted. If Ray were smiling, his face would brighten with deep dimples, but there's no smiling today. He's being comforted and stroked by Beth. She's now in a peach ensemble that brightens her complexion.

"Ray, she's a fighter. You know she's a fighter."

Ray nods, but he's inconsolable.

Beth continues as she strokes his arm. "They said moderate A.D.R....or whatever it's called...but they did use the term 'moderate.' That's got to be good news."

Ray speaks in a low monotone, as if he hasn't yet processed it all, "A.R.D.S., Adult Respiratory Distress Syndrome. Bruised lungs." Ray drops his head into his hands. "God, just let her be all right."

Kate's spirit floats very close to Ray's face and whispers, "I'm fine, honey, just fine."

No acknowledgment from Ray. He drops his head. Beth puts her arm around him and pats his shoulder. The spirit rests on Beth's peach silk-covered arm. "Tell him, Beth. Tell him I'm going to be all right."

Kate's spirit is now drawn hurriedly down the corridor. Patients in wheelchairs and on gurneys pass below in a blur. Kate closes her eyes and scrunches up in anticipation of hitting the wall at the end of the hallway. Instead, she glides effortlessly through the outside wall.

The afternoon sunshine startles Kate, but it's only a moment before she is whooshed into a long darkened tunnel, then, just as suddenly, catapulted through to blinding, eye-stinging light.

In a flash, Kate's airy form with Kate's facial features falls softly to recline in a magnificent, lush green valley of oversized blossoms in amazing, electric shades of brilliant teal, sunset orange and neon fuchsia. The colors are almost liquid, melting into one another. The blooms are vivid and appear outlined, as if being viewed through 3-D glasses. Kate luxuriates in the carpet-like grass.

A spirit with an elderly countenance and a sweet welcoming smile, dressed in a hooded pewter gray gown, flutters toward Kate. Kate looks up, astonished. "Nanny!" she says. "Oh, Nanny, I've missed you. Where are we? This place is so incredibly beautiful!"

Nanny's elderly spirit shimmers next to Kate. Kate leans into the spirit, warming at the contact. She smiles broadly. "Nanny, I've missed you so."

"Darlin', I've missed you, too, but you can't stay."

Kate pouts. Her bottom lip goes out and her chin quivers. "Why not? I want to stay here with you."

Spirit Nanny abruptly floats upward, suddenly all business. "It's not your time."

Kate sulks.

Nanny's spirit continues, "Hate to rush you, honey, but you really do need to get a move on. They'll be resuscitating you soon back in the hospital and Marilyn's waiting to accompany you back."

Kate questions, "Marilyn? Who's Marilyn? Why can't you take me back?"

"Marilyn handles returns, honey. You need to get going, and I'm late already for Canasta with Eleanor Roosevelt, your cousin Ben, and John Belushi."

Kate questions, "Marilyn? Do you mean Aunt Marilyn?"

Nanny's spirit pulsates in place, "Oh, no, no, dear. You need a lot of experience to handle returns. Your Aunt Marilyn's only been here since '94. This Marilyn's a sweet little spirit who's been around since the early sixties. You'd better get going. Ray and your little beauties are waiting."

Kate smiles as Nanny continues, "Send a heavenly hug to your Mother for me. Honey, we will be together again some day, I promise." Nanny floats off and then darts back momentarily. "Everything in its own time, darlin'."

Kate shouts, "I love you, Nanny!"

Nanny shouts back, "And I love you too, my little Sweet Cakes."

Kate's lip quivers again. "No one has called me that for years."

At that very moment, a glowing, gauzy figure darts in and circles Kate. The spirit, with a pretty face and the delicate features, vaguely familiar, of a woman in her mid-thirties, leans into Kate. "I'm Marilyn, Kate. Nice to meet you." Before Kate can acknowledge Marilyn, she continues, "Better run now. Please, mortals first."

Spirit Marilyn lightly blows on Kate's gown and they both twirl up in the vortex that spins on the hilltop, swaying perfect blades of grass. Kate and Spirit Marilyn dart out of the vortex and float over vibrant turquoise streams and deep teal hillsides the exact shade of Kate's patio umbrella. Kate speaks in a reverent tone, like she's in church. "It is soooo gloriously beautiful here! What incredible, astonishing color and beauty!"

Marilyn says softly, "It's reflecting the beauty you have inside."

Kate is touched. She replies, "Why, that's just about the nicest thing anyone has ever said to me."

Marilyn smiles broadly, "Thanks. I liked it too when they first told me that. I took quite a beating on earth, so I felt proud that I could reflect any beauty at all."

They float without speaking, passing spiraling crystal steeples, angled rooftops of shimmering mosaic tiles, and pastures with intricate crop circle designs. Kate marvels at the intensity of the experience.

Marilyn turns back toward Kate as she takes a deep breath. Kate darts behind Marilyn in an attempt to avoid the tornado effect she suspects is about to sweep her up and away. Marilyn laughs. "Not quite yet. I was just feeling the intensity of the experience, like you are. I love this part of the trip back."

"Do you provide this escort service pretty often?" Kate inquires.

"Not as often as I'd like. Sometimes the call from loved ones on earth is so strong that inductees are sent back."

"Is that what happened with me?"

"Sounds like a whole lot of love was bouncing off the walls of that long dark tunnel, calling you back to life, right before you entered the white light," Marilyn explains. "And you have a purpose to fulfill."

They float for what seems like hours, but is actually more like seconds. Kate is so taken by the extreme beauty that surrounds her that she hardly notices Marilyn taking another deep breath. At the last minute, she tries to move out of the path, but Spirit Marilyn outsmarts her and turns, blowing out a great gust of air in Kate's direction. Kate loses her balance in midair and tumbles down in free fall, then slows abruptly just inches before hitting the ground to come to rest softly on a grassy hilltop. She can't help but stretch for a moment in the plush, almost furry grass. She shouts up at Marilyn, "Is this the hill from *The Sound of Music*? It looks just like it did in Technicolor!" Kate looks around and adds, "Well, except there

24

are no Austrian Alps."

Spirit Marilyn just flutters.

Kate moans. "So this is it? You take me to the edge of town and then I get to ride a windstorm home?"

Marilyn's Spirit nods from above and then puckers up and blows lightly toward Kate.

Kate tumbles down the hill from the force of the breeze. She scoffs, "And you need years of experience to help with returns? Seems like anyone could do this! Just pucker up and blow."

Unable to control herself, Kate builds up momentum on the long fall and tumbles in giant summersaults down the hillside. The moment she hits bottom...

Spirit Kate is back in the hospital room, floating near the ceiling. She watches the frenzy of activity around her body lying still on the hospital bed below but with a definite rise and fall of the chest. The crisis has passed, blood pressure readings appear stabilized on the monitor, and the patient's body temperature is back to normal. Kate can tell that she has actually been gone only a few moments because the dark-haired female doctor has just placed the paddles back on the cart and the nurse with the teddy bear scrubs is rolling it out of the room. The doctor writes something on the chart and also leaves.

Ray, who has been waiting outside in the hallway, rushes in and stands by the bed. He has been crying. The light in the room has been dimmed, which makes Kate look even more pale and sickly. Ray studies Kate's face and gently strokes her cheek, then sits down in a chair next to the bed and stares at the floor, bent with worry and grief.

The spirit of Kate floats slowly down from the ceiling and drifts like a beautiful bubble over to where Ray is sitting. She bumps him gently a few times, as though to get his attention, but he is too absorbed in his thoughts to notice, and too filled with worry for her to penetrate. Spirit Kate hovers near Ray for a moment, observing him compassionately, then turns and floats over to her own body on the bed. She tries to push and squeeze herself back into her body, but no luck. It's too tight. She tries going in from the side. No go. Finally, unsure what to try next, she rests for a moment on top of her body, waiting for inspiration, and suddenly realizes she is already back in her body, as though she had just sunk or melted into herself. The color immediately returns to Kate's face, but Ray doesn't notice. He's still staring at the floor, preoccupied with his own thoughts.

Hours later, Kate is tossing and turning on the hospital bed. Her eyes open. It's dark in the room except for the thin strip of lighting over her head. Kate asks weakly, "Ray, are you there?" There's no answer.

There is motion in the room as someone leans over Kate. Kate's eyes try to focus on a nametag. It's on a white dress looming over her—a very low-cut white dress that barely contains the cleavage within. The nametag says "Norma Jean B...a..."—is that a "k"? Kate shuts her eyes and opens them again slowly. Now she can see the nametag more clearly: It says "Norma Jean Baker."

The nurse straightens and stands next to the bed. Instead of a nurse's uniform or scrubs, she wears a soft, white, form-fitting Grecian-style dress with a deep V-neckline halter top. The nurse is Marilyn Monroe. An imaginary subway grate

26

blows air from the floor, billowing the accordion pleating on her dress, like the renowned scene from *The Seven Year Itch*.

Kate questions weakly, "Norma...Jean...Baker? Norma Jean Baker?! Marilyn Monroe?!!"

Marilyn nods.

"You're sure dressed up for the night shift," Kate says.

Marilyn responds, "My Sunday best! You go with what you know, I guess."

Kate smiles and then closes her eyes.

Kate opens her eyes. The morning sunlight is streaming through the windows and there is a lot of activity in the room. A stooped lady empties the wastebasket, and a nurse in green scrubs checks the monitors. A breakfast tray sits next to the bed.

Kate winces only slightly as Ray, sitting right next to her bed, excitedly grabs her hand, squeezing the IV tube. Ray squeals in his hushed hospital tone, "She's awake. Nurse, she's awake!"

The nurse leans over. Kate pulls at her scrubs. "Where's the white dress?" The nurse straightens up. It's not Marilyn Monroe; it's an older lady with crinkly short gray hair. "Well, hello, sleepyhead, and if you came in wearing a white dress, dear, it should be hanging in the closet." Kate is clearly disappointed. "Where's Marilyn?"

The nurse looks around the room and answers, "Sorry, no Marilyn here, but I'm Ruth. Will I do?" Before Kate can answer, Ruth goes on. "Are you ready for some light breakfast? And your very nice gentleman caller has been waiting patiently for you to awaken."

Kate speaks slowly, as she finds talking very taxing.

"Marilyn...was...my nurse...last...night." Kate quickly fades.

Ray looks expectantly at the nurse, "Now that's a good sign, right, that she's alert and talkative?"

Ruth nods. "You're right, young man. That's a very good sign. She's come around quicker than we expected, but she'll be fading in and out for a while." She lowers her voice conspiratorially. "And that business about Marilyn and the white dress, don't let that bother you. She may be a little confused at first between dreams and reality."

Later that morning, Kate is sound asleep in her bed. She's alone in the room. When she stirs, Marilyn Monroe is immediately at her side, stroking her cheek. Marilyn is now wearing a white dress in a scattered cherry print. It has a deep V-neckline, soft ties on either shoulder, and an exaggerated cinched waistline.

Kate opens her eyes and sighs loudly. "I wasn't hallucinating. It is you. Marilyn Mon-freakin'-roe! Unbelievable!" Kate inspects Marilyn's dress. "Let me guess. This one's from *The Misfits*?"

Marilyn nods.

"Funny," Kate adds. "I never was a big fan, sorry, no offense."

Marilyn counters, "No offense taken."

"But I sure remember that dress, and the white one from *The Seven Year Itch*. Guess they made more of an emotional connection than I thought."

Marilyn shakes her head lightly. "More likely it was because the studio publicity department was earning their keep," Marilyn responds. "Making sure everybody in America saw stills of me in those dresses. I sure posed enough in each costume I ever wore."

Kate smiles. "You were, er, are so beautiful."

"Thanks. She was pretty, wasn't she?" Marilyn replies.

"She?" Kate questions.

"This Marilyn Monroe creature," Marilyn responds, almost dreamily. "Wish I could have really felt beautiful, inside and out."

Kate licks her lips. "Ooh, dry mouth!"

Marilyn grabs a glass and a small plastic pitcher, then pours a half glass of water. She pops a bendable hospital straw into the glass and then gingerly hands the water to Kate. Like a curious child, Kate bends the straw up and down a few times, then takes a big sip, then another, and another, before setting the glass down on the tray next to the bed. She waits a moment, and then bends the straw again, just for good measure. "Got any Darvon, Marilyn?"

Marilyn shrugs. She pats her dress where pockets would be if she had any, shakes her head no, and adds, "Sorry. Unlike my last time on earth, I have no drugs of any kind."

Kate shakes her head no, mocking Marilyn. She grabs the side of her head. "Ooh. That hurt!"

Marilyn can't help but chuckle. "And you thought tumbling down the hill was going to hurt."

Kate is shocked. "The hill! Sorry, I'm not putting things together very well yet. I'm still a little fuzzy here, and I'm not quite sure where I am at any given moment or what day it is..." Marilyn answers in the exaggerated tones of an announcer, "It's Interior Hospital Room, Sunday, August 1, 1999, eleven oh three in the morning." Kate smiles. "Why, thank you." Marilyn responds, "I do a little better in script form." Kate starts to laugh, then stops suddenly in obvious distress. "Ooh, don't want to press my luck with my lungs." She pauses for breath, then continues more cautiously, "So are you Marilyn, er...Norma, the spirit Nanny introduced me to, from..." she lowers her voice "...the *other* side?"

Marilyn nods. "One and the same, but actually I prefer Norma. And I'm here to help you with the transition back to earth."

Kate scowls. "Ooh! Now I feel bad for complaining about the escort to the hilltop. This is pretty good customer service after all. Of course, it's not like returning a blender to Macy's, but I wouldn't expect anything less than perfect service from actual heaven!" Kate tries to keep her eyes open, but she is losing the battle. Her eyes close. She whispers, "Sorry, I'm fading fast."

Norma runs her hand lightly over Kate's brow. Kate half opens one eye. "How long can you stay?" Norma responds softly, "My last trip back was a few years ago and I stayed almost a whole day but..."

Kate interrupts, "Norma, will I ever be the same?" Norma reassures Kate. "Of course you will. This will pass, and you'll go back to being a wife and mother and lawyer and friend and..."

There's a loud clanking sound from the hallway. Norma says, "Guess they'll be bringing in your lunch tray soon." Kate says faintly, "Lunch? Didn't I just have breakfast?" and that quickly, she's out again.

Norma runs her hand lightly across Kate's cheek. "Just rest, baby girl. I've finally found you, and this time I won't let you go."

Chapter Three

Recognition

Ray enters Kate's hospital room. Kate jumps out of bed and meets him at the door with a big kiss. Ray gasps. "Wow! Guess I don't have to ask how you're feeling today! They said you were doing great, but this is a pleasant surprise." Kate floats around the room, holding the sleeves of her paisley robe like butterfly wings. "I feel terrific! I'm out of that dreary hospital gown and I'm freshly showered and shampooed and Doctor Sloane said that I won't have any residual damage at all. My lungs are fine, and I'm fine." Kate looks behind Ray. "Where are the kids? I can't wait to get my hands on them."

Ray gently guides her to the hospital bed and lowers her to a seated position. "The kids are with Beth and they'll be here soon. But you'd better not get overtired. You really had us worried there for a while."

"That's all behind us now," she says playfully. Kate shakes her arm in front of him. "Look, I'm not plugged in! Wanna walk the halls for a change of scenery?" Kate steers Ray through the door and out into the hallway before he has a chance to answer or protest.

Kate and Ray walk hand-in-hand around oversized food carts. Ray stops for a moment. "It's almost lunch time. Are you sure you want to walk now?"

Kate leans in, "Believe me, the applesauce isn't going anywhere. They'll just bring it in again for my afternoon snack, and I'll surprise them this time by being awake."

They stop momentarily at the nurses' station, where Ray speaks in confidence to a young nurse with Pippi Longstocking braids. He rejoins Kate and gives her a thumbs-up while tying the sash on her robe. He guides her down the hall and into the elevator. Kate shivers with excitement. "We're busting out!"

The busy cafeteria has close-ups of fruits and vegetables laminated on the lime-green walls. Ray helps Kate get settled at a booth for two. "How about a vanilla milkshake?" he asks.

Kate shivers. "Sounds great! And a piece of pie!"

Ray nods enthusiastically. "A shake and pie it is." He walks to the counter and gets in line.

Kate looks around the cafeteria and focuses her attention on a curly-haired toddler as he alternates between inhaling Cheerios and putting his Daddy's keys in his mouth. He sees Kate looking at him and gives her a big smile. He's so cute she can't help laughing.

She gets up and joins Ray in line, apologizing to those in line behind him. She gives Ray a big hug and then selects a sliver of cherry pie. Ray is getting his change from the cashier as Kate asks, "How about my movie star nurse?"

Ray shoots her a blank look. "Ruth reminds you of a movie star? Who, Olympia Dukakis?"

"Not Ruth, silly, Marilyn, er, Norma."

Ray is puzzled. "Who are Marilyn and Norma? From the night shift? And speaking of nurses, we signed the Accident Release. Surely we don't need a nurse coming home with us. I mean...uh...unless you think we do. What do you think? Of course, if you want a nurse, then by all means... "

"Norma's coming home with us?" Kate asks excitedly as she careens out of the cafeteria. Ray abandons the vanilla shake and the cherry pie on the tray and rushes off after her. The crowd shoots him sympathetic glances. One big guy says to Ray as he races by, "Been there, done that!"

Kate rushes into her hospital room. Ruth is standing by the door, adding notes to the white board. Kate rushes past her to check in the bathroom and the closet, and then under the bed. Ruth asks, "Looking for something, dear?"

Ray enters the room as Kate scooches out from under the bed. She stays kneeling. "Yes, I'm looking for my nurse, Norma. She might be hiding since there's so much activity around here."

Ruth looks at Ray and gently shakes her head. "Norma, did you say? Why, we haven't had a nurse named Norma on this floor for years. There was Norma Milton three or four years back and Norma Turner about ten years ago. I doubt that either of them would be under your bed, dear."

Kate interrupts, "Yes, this Norma must be new here. Norma Baker's my nurse. She looks just like Marilyn Monroe."

Ruth giggles as she helps Kate to bed. "Yes, and our Chief of Surgery is a dead ringer for Clark Gable. You must meet him, dear, after your nap." In spite of Kate's protestations, Ruth gets her settled in the bed. Ray is at Kate's side. "Honey, don't overexert yourself. It'll take a while for you to get back up to speed. Let's not rush it."

Ruth interjects, "Dear, do you know how long you've been in the hospital?"

Kate sleepily answers, "Since last night?" Kate hesitates a moment, "No, must've been the night before because Norma had on the dress from *The Misfits* yesterday. The night before was *The Seven Year Itch* dress."

Ruth nods knowingly, "Right, dear." She rolls her eyes at Ray. "Now, let's get you comfortable," Ruth says as she fluffs the pillow.

In seconds, Kate is asleep.

Kate slowly awakens. She's groggy from the morning's activity. She moves aside the bed table, ignoring the lunch tray with its obligatory cup of applesauce. Norma, in the emerald-green dance hall girl costume from *Bus Stop* with its over-the-top fish-scale print, netting and tassels and the ratty fishnet hose, stands at the foot of the bed, staring at the small TV.

"Hi, hon. You've missed the most exciting show about cross-dressers married to sisters. I mean sisters like ex-nuns, not brothers and sisters."

Kate grimaces. "Daytime TV is so enlightening." Both women giggle. Then Kate gets serious. "Norma, I need to ask you about..."

A portly male aide wearing a hair net enters the room and walks right through Norma to pick up the food tray. He asks, "Doing OK this afternoon, Mrs. Davis? You don't seem to have much of an appetite." When he doesn't get an answer, he looks up from the food tray. Kate is visibly shaken. The aide stammers, "Do we n-n-need a nurse in here?"

Kate looks right at Norma. "No, thanks. I already have one."

The aide grabs the food tray and hurries out. Norma sits next to Kate on the edge of the bed. Kate extends her arm straight out and runs it through Norma. She then sinks back into her bed and squeezes her eyes shut. Kate slowly opens her eyes. Marilyn is still there. She says softly, "Still here?"

Norma begins, "Kate, I'm real, but I can only be seen and heard by you."

Kate distractedly twirls her hair as she speaks, "My nurse, well, Ruth, my real nurse, was worried that I was confused about the days but she needn't have worried. I have it clear in my head now. Today must be Monday. Yeah, Kurt Cobain visits on Friday, on Saturday it's Winston Churchill, Michael Landon on Sunday, and Marilyn Monroe on Monday."

Norma jumps up from the bed and hurriedly shoves aside Kate's plants, Beanie Babies and cards from the windowsill, then hops up on it and takes a seat. "We'll talk later. You have visitors."

Beth, in coordinated orange sorbet-colored camp shirt and shorts, enters with Kate's twins. Beth has dressed the twins in their smocked tops, normally reserved for holiday photos. Beth claps, "OK, jump on her, kids!" Blaire and Brady are an auburn-smocked blur as they both race to Kate's lap. They all kiss, hug and exchange greetings.

Beth opens her purse and takes out a giant chocolate bar. She waves the candy bar back and forth under Kate's nose. "I've brought chocolate." When there's hardly a response from Kate, she lightly pinches Kate's cheek. "Hey, lady, anybody home in there? I said chocolate."

Kate smiles weakly.

"Kate, you're so pale. Looks like you've seen a ghost."

"I have," Kate answers.

Beth's eyes dart around the room.

Blaire and Brady admire an assortment of shiny metallic

helium "Get Well" balloons tied to the window latch. Norma sits very close to the kids, watching intently as they poke the balloons. Blaire actually leans her arm against Norma's leg while reaching for a particularly enticing balloon with Bart Simpson proudly writing "Get Well Soon" over and over on the blackboard. Norma leans close to Blaire and takes in the scent of Johnson's Baby Shampoo.

Kate says softly, "I had a near death experience."

Beth asks in a low, secretive tone, "Really? Like on the old *Donahue* show, with the tunnel and the white light?"

Kate nods.

"Ooh, tell me all. I'm *dying* to hear." Beth looks around the room anxiously. "Well, not literally. Gotta be careful what you say around here."

Norma laughs as Ray enters the hospital room. He kisses Kate. "Beth, doesn't our patient look wonderful today?" Beth agrees. "I was just telling her how great her color looks." Kate looks at Beth and shakes her head.

Beth jumps up. "Hey, kiddoes. Wanna go upstairs and see the babies?"

The kids screech in delight. "Daddy see the babies?"

Ray waves the way to the door. "Sounds like a great idea to me." Beth and the kids follow. Ray gently guides Beth back to the chair next to Kate's bed. "I'll take them, Beth. Why don't you and Kate have a nice visit?"

"Are you sure you're okay with that?" Beth asks coyly.

"Of course," Ray reassures her.

Kate laughs. "Ray, isn't it funny how Beth was able to get you to think this was your idea?"

Norma gets down from the windowsill and squats next to Beth, comparing bustlines. She holds her costume even tighter against her chest, and then straightens. Norma turns to face Kate, "No contest." Kate grins.

Norma joins Ray and the kids at the door. "I'm going with them. I'd love to see the babies."

Ray turns back to Kate, "Try to stay awake till we get back."

Norma, Ray and the kids leave the room. They're barely out the door before Beth pulls her chair right next to Kate's bed. "So, what gives?"

"Beth, during this near death experience, I saw Nanny. It was SO incredible!"

Beth holds the tray table to steady herself. "Did you ask her for any lottery numbers?"

Ray, the twins and Norma join a bevy of proud new parents, siblings and grandparents stationed at the nursery window. Each leans against the glass and coos at their own baby out of the dozen sleeping or squealing babies inside the nursery. Ray bends down to the twins' eye level. "The boy babies are wrapped in blue blankets, and the little girls are in pink."

Baby Boy Patterson is very unhappy. He arches his back and cries out in a loud shriek. His red-faced cry is heard through the glass.

Blaire's lip quivers. "Blue baby cryin'."

Ray consoles her. "Maybe he's hungry, or just missing his Mommy and Daddy. The nurse will check on him, honey."

As if on cue, the nurse tightens the blanket cocoon around Baby Boy Patterson but it doesn't help. He still cries out and the nurse moves on to another baby in need.

Norma "pops" through the glass window into the nursery

and puts a pacifier from Baby Boy Patterson's isolette into his little fingers and then guides it to his mouth. Ray is astonished as he watches the newborn baby seemingly position his own pacifier. Before Ray can check more closely, Baby Boy Patterson spits out the pacifier. He is not comforted. He twitches and fusses.

Brady watches intently through the glass as the nurse again tends to Baby Boy Patterson. She turns him onto his stomach, which doesn't quiet him. The baby draws up his legs and squeals and keeps crying. The nurse is frustrated. "Poor little crack baby," she says in a whisper.

Norma flattens her hand against the baby's back, applying slight pressure. The baby immediately stops crying.

Norma "pops" back through the glass and stands by Ray. She lightly strokes Brady's neck. Brady feels the touch. He flips his hand at the back of his neck, as if to shoo away a fly.

Norma pops through the door marked "No entry. Cardiac ICU" and stops at the nurses' station. She glances at a chart lying on the counter. "OK, Madelyn Phillips, Room 122, let's rock and roll."

An alarm sounds. A nurse jumps up from the station, "Code blue!" A second nurse turns off the alarm and shouts, "Paddles for 122!"

In Room 122, Madelyn, an elderly woman hooked up to cables and wires from every orifice, half-opens her eyes as Norma stands nearby. Norma manifests as an elderly man in a worn sport coat and slacks. Madelyn smiles. She slurs, "Harvey? I knew you'd come for me."

Norma walks quickly to the bed and leans in close. She speaks in a man's deep but raspy baritone. "Let's go home, Maddie. We'll go toward the light together."

Maddie beams. The jagged mountaintop shapes on her monitor flat line and the buzzing in the room becomes a persistent, high volume monotone.

The medical team rushes into Madelyn's room with the crash cart just as Maddie and Norma, both gauzy-gowned spirits, float into the hallway.

Spirits Maddie and Norma hover in the clouds, waiting in Heaven's Incoming Processing Line. Norma moves out of line and glides over to Peg, the spirit in charge of Admissions, with a pencil stuck into her hood. Peg checks incoming on her clipboard.

"Back so soon, Norma? Have you spoken with Kate yet about your relationship and her future?"

Norma shrugs. "No, not yet. We haven't had a moment that seemed appropriate, but I will. I'm just escorting one through. It's Madelyn Phillips. Her husband, Harvey will be waiting to welcome her. I'll be going right back."

Peg points her pencil at Norma. "Time's running out, Norma. You have to return soon. Only a short time left to get Kate prepared for her future. She has a tough road ahead."

A spirit floats over to Peg and frantically circles her. Exasperated, Peg turns to leave. "Sorry, Norma. Duty calls. You know how it is. There's no rest in Admissions, but please keep me posted. I'm on nights this week." Peg floats away, then turns back momentarily. "Look to the heavens, hon. If I'm blinking, I'm in.

HELLO, NORMA JEAN

Chapter Four

A Friend In Need

Beth is drained. She leans over Kate's tray table. "This is fucking unbelievable. Can your gauzy little spirit nurse tell you things that are about to happen?"

"I don't know." Kate answers. "Marilyn, I mean Norma, hasn't said what her powers are."

Beth shudders. "So you have a ghost with an identity crisis! Norma, Marilyn? What difference does it make?"

Kate corrects her. "She just prefers to be called Norma."

The light goes on for Beth. "Norma. Marilyn. Holy shit! Is your vision in gauze Marilyn Monroe?"

Kate nods.

Beth jumps up and paces the room. "My God! Drew's such a fan. Remember when we had that big fight because he paid seventy-five bucks for that old *Playboy* with Marilyn on the cover?"

Norma "pops" through the wall and Beth paces right through her. Norma says, "That was the very first *Playboy*!" Kate says to Norma, "Was it really the very first *Playboy*?" Beth stops momentarily, thinking Kate is addressing her. "That's what Drew said, but he would've said anything to justify seventy-five dollars for an old magazine."

Beth rants, "Back to more important issues, just think of the possibilities. Was it the C.I.A. or an overdose when she died back in—what was it—nineteen sixty something?" Beth plops down in the chair. Norma stands right in front of her. Beth takes a quick breath and then she's off again, "Was Yves Montand a great lover? Was Jack insatiable? Was it really Bobby she loved?"

Norma shakes her head. "Does she go on like this all the time?"

Kate shakes her head up and down emphatically. "Absolutely."

"You think so?" Beth asks. "I don't know what I believe, but I'd sure love to know first-hand." Beth stops for a moment.

"Finished, Beth?" Kate inquires.

Beth quickly responds, "Finished? I'm just getting started. Did she really love only Arthur Miller, and what about Joe DiMaggio? Talk about carrying a torch! I remember reading that he left a dozen roses on her grave every week for like twenty years!"

Kate interjects, "Do you really care?"

Beth doesn't even acknowledge Kate as she continues, "Do you think she and Marlon Brando ever..."

Norma giggles.

Beth stops momentarily. "Jesus! She generates more heat dead than most of us do alive. Ooh, wish I could see her."

Kate laughs. "You're looking right at her."

Beth reddens. "Are you kidding? She's here right now? Where?" Beth pokes her arm out and touches Norma's ass.

Norma giggles, "Fresh!"

Beth moves her hand and fans the *Bus Stop* costume's tassels across Norma's hip.

Kate smiles. "Sorry, she said only I can see or hear her."

Norma stands right in front of Beth and clenches to try and manifest herself to Beth. No luck. She pushes harder, her face reddening. As Beth stares straight ahead, a thick haze forms and slowly takes shape. It's more and more defined. It's a woman's body...definitely a woman's body. It's a knockout woman's body, now in the bright pink strapless dress from *Gentlemen Prefer Blondes*.

Beth gasps. "It's Marilyn Monroe!" Beth adds, "Ma-ter-i-al Girl," mocking Madonna's video.

Marilyn looks puzzled. She corrects Beth. "No, 'Diamonds Are a Girl's Best Friend.' " Beth is apologetic. "No, a singer memorialized you in her music video and it was..."

Norma squeals, playfully mocking herself as Lorelei Lee in *Gentlemen Prefer Blondes*. "Ooh! What's a music video?" With an exaggerated pouty mouth, Norma continues. "Beth, you asked more questions in your little session just now than I was asked during my last stay in the psychiatric clinic."

Beth instinctively touches Norma's bulging cleavage. "Christ! Are those real?" She laughs, "I brought candy to a sick friend and I'm feeling up Marilyn Monroe!"

Norma corrects her. "Call me Norma. All my new friends do."

Beth laughs nervously. "Norma, it's so great to meet you and we have tons of questions."

Kate balks. "We? I beg your pardon. You're the one with all the questions."

Norma says, "I'll gladly tell you all my secrets, Beth, if you tell me yours. You go first."

Beth is shocked. "Secrets? How exciting could our secrets be?"

Norma paces deliberately around the room. "Oh, I don't know. How about we start with Tim, the paralegal in contracts with your firm."

The ladies are impressed. Beth stands tall. "I'm game. Nothing like playing 'tit' for tat with Marilyn Monroe."

Norma is genuinely tickled.

Kate corrects Norma, "Don't encourage her," and then corrects Beth, "You mean tit for tat with Norma Jean Baker."

Beth stands corrected. "OK, Norma. Sorry to disappoint you, but mine's not much of a secret. So far, Tim's just an innocent flirtation; maybe because my husband hasn't touched me in six months."

Kate grimaces. "No interest even when she was practically nude on their dining room table."

Norma turns and throws Beth a questioning look, "You were what?"

"Tell the smorgasbord story," Kate implores.

Beth doesn't need to be asked twice. She pours a little of Kate's water into a glass and downs a quick swig. "Right before Drew was due home one evening when the kids were at their Granny's, I got real inventive and just climbed right onto our antique dining table. Here I was in a reclining position, wearing the highest of spiked heels and the tiniest of panties. I had strategically placed a little bowl of dip here (she points to the area between her breasts) and another in the nether region."

"Martha Stewart, eat your heart out," Kate interjects.

Beth continues, "I artistically trailed bite-sized carrots, celery, broccoli and cauliflower to the dip. While waiting, I sampled the dip. It was great." Beth takes a deep breath and forges ahead, "When Drew arrived, he came into the kitchen to check the mail. I called out to him to come into the dining room. He stood in the entryway looking as crisp and fresh as he had at seven-thirty that morning...oh, except that he had loosened his tie. Anyway, barely glancing my way he reached for a carrot stick, swirled it in the bowl nestled in my cleavage and then turned and left the room."

Norma cringes. "Ouch! That hurts."

Kate counters, "As if that wasn't enough, he ends it by shouting back that he had salad for lunch."

"Bet that's not all he had for lunch," Beth adds.

"Kind of sad, don't you think?" inquires Norma. Before they can answer, Ray and the twins enter in a rush.

Blaire runs to Kate. "Babies cryin', Mama."

Kate soothes her. "Maybe they were just hungry, darlin'. I'm sure they're fine now, right, Daddy?"

Ray agrees. "Right. They were crying for their bottles."

Beth roots through her purse. "I'm kinda hungry myself. Wish I had somebody to go with me to get a snack. There's a vending machine down by the waiting room."

Ray says, "You're not suckering me into this one." Beth laughs. "No, honestly. I could use a treat. Anybody want a little goodie?" Blaire and Brady look to Kate. "Can we, Mommy?" Blaire asks.

"Sure, but only a granola bar." The twins run to Beth.

Beth says, "You heard your Mommy, kids. Two Reese's peanut butter cups coming up." She asks Ray and Kate, "Anything for you?"

Kate answers, "No, thanks." Ray pats Kate's hand. "We have everything we need, thanks."

Beth takes the kids by the hand. "Let's go, kids. Sounds like we're trapped in a Hallmark card in here." She turns back to Kate and Ray, "We'll be right back." Beth turns and waves to Norma.

Ray says, "Your aim is a little off, Beth. We're over here!"

Beth smiles and waves in their direction, then walks out the door with the kids. Beth leans back in, "No heavy petting. Looks like Chachi's coming this way."

Kate smiles. "Doctor Sloane does look like Scott Baio."

There's a light tapping on the door and then a young male doctor who resembles Scott Baio enters the room. Ray asks, "More good news, Doctor Sloane?"

The doctor replies, "Well, actually, Mr. and Mrs. Davis, it's great news. Our patient can go home tomorrow."

Ray and Kate cheer.

Kate inquires, "No residual effects, right?"

"Right. Your pulmonary function test results were fine."

"So I aced the test."

"Well, you should recover almost all of your lung function in three or four months."

"Oh. Okay. Anything else?"

The doctor consults the chart. "Yes, in three months or so you should be finished with the morning sickness."

Kate and Ray are ashen.

Kate lifts the sheet and stares at her flat stomach. "Holy shit! Another baby."

Chapter Five

Old Friends

The only light in Kate's hospital room emanates from the TV screen. Norma, in the off-the-shoulder black dress from *Asphalt Jungle*, watches late night TV as Kate stares straight ahead. Norma mutes the TV. "I'm a good listener."

"I'm sure you are, but I'm playing Scarlett O'Hara right now. I'll just worry about this tomorrow. Ray really wants this baby, but I don't know." Kate smiles. "Go ahead and turn the sound back on. I know how much you enjoy TV. It's not bothering me."

Norma turns up the TV sound as Shelley Winters tells a story to Conan O'Brien. Norma gasps. "Shelley Winters! Can you believe it? She and I were roommates at the Hollywood Studio Club when we were starting out." On the screen, Shelley follows Conan's gaze to her ample chest. He feigns embarrassment as the audience snickers. They're all in on the joke. Shelley leans toward Conan. "Like my...pearls?" Conan's eyes sparkle. The audience loves it. Norma laughs. "She always was such a character."

Norma turns to Kate, "Do you need anything?"

"No, thanks. I'm going to get some sleep."

Norma turns off the TV. She speaks in a low voice, "Rest

easy. I'll be back soon. I need to check something down the hall." Norma "pops" through the wall.

Norma "pops" into the doctors' quarters where the interns and residents grab some shut-eye. Three of the four bunks in the sparse room are occupied. Two doctors are sound asleep; the third, a young man in a white V-neck T-shirt and green scrub pants, tosses and turns. Norma stands in the shadows by his lower bunk. She's in the gold lamé dress with the plunging V-neckline that she wore in *Gentlemen Prefer Blondes*.

Norma walks slowly toward Todd, the young intern.

Todd plumps his pillow and turns on his side. Moments later he lifts his head up and looks right through Norma at the wall clock. He groans, "Man! Due on the floor in an hour." Frustrated, he punches his pillow and flips over on his back.

Norma stands very near and leans in close to Todd, their faces almost touching. She moves slowly, deliberately. Todd instinctively turns toward her. His clenched face visibly relaxes as Norma moves her soft hair across his forehead. Todd lazily runs his hand across his face and moans. As she leans across him, Todd smiles broadly.

Norma stands and moves back from the bunk. Todd is contented, relaxed. She whispers, "Rest easy."

Norma walks to the window and looks through the blinds up into the night sky. She focuses on a rapidly blinking star. "I know, Peg, but she's been through a lot. Maybe tomorrow." The star blinks nonstop. "Stop it. I may not even tell her about our connection or what's ahead for her with Ray. I haven't decided yet." The star continues to blink. Norma turns her back to the window. "Blink, blink, blink to you, too. No need for sarcasm, Peg."

A fortyish nurse with curly hair barely being contained by a wide headband enters Kate's empty hospital room. There are loud sobs coming from the bathroom. The nurse taps on the bathroom door. "Okay in there, Miss Davis?"

Kate comes out of the bathroom. She's being propped up on one side by Norma, who's in the white strapless dress with the big flower at her waist from *All About Eve*.

The nurse only sees that Kate's left arm is hanging at a very peculiar angle because Norma is bracing her. The nurse immediately pushes in under Kate's left arm and helps her to bed. Norma then moves around to Kate's right arm and braces it.

"Have you hurt your arm, Miss Davis?" the nurse asks. "Can I get you anything?"

Norma leans in, "Maybe just some privacy."

Kate says curtly, "Norma!"

The nurse answers, "Sorry, it's Tracey."

Kate answers the nurse. "Nothing, thanks, Tracey. I'm okay. I just needed a good cry."

The nurse escorts Kate back to her bed. "If you're sure then, I'll leave you alone." Tracey hands Kate a tissue and puts the call button next to her pillow. "You just let me know if you need anything," she continues. She exits the room.

Kate pulls the sheet over her face, then pulls it off and sits up. "I was just getting comfortable with seeing Nanny and meeting you and then..." Her voice trails off.

Norma states, "Perfectly normal reaction, Kate. We see it all the time. Just try to relax."

Kate shudders. "And now...the baby." She breaks down crying again. Between sobs and sniffs, Norma can make out only "three babies...under three...years old...already thirty-seven." Kate hugs her knees up close to her chest. Norma sits down on the bed next to Kate and puts her arms around her, gently rocking her. "Let someone else be strong for you." Norma hugs her close.

Kate is sitting on her bed in this upright fetal position when Tracey enters the room with a tray holding a cup of ice, a Ginger Ale and a plate of breakfast food. She races to Kate's side. "Are you cramping?"

Kate straightens. "No. Just trying to get comfortable."

Tracey puts the items down on the tray table and slides it over Kate's bed. Norma leans in to smell the bacon. She picks up a slice and immediately drops it back on the plate. "Whew! I thought I missed bacon. It smells funny."

Kate fires back. "It smells fine!"

Tracey questions, "It does? Well, good." She eases toward the door. "Unless you'll be needing something then?"

Before Kate can even answer, the nurse is out the door.

Norma hands Kate a fork. "Better eat fast. The cute young doctor's releasing you today."

"Not if I'm cramping and crying and sniffing fake bacon."

"Fake bacon?" Norma inquires.

Kate again picks up the perfectly formed bacon and shakes it at Norma. "Well, Sizzlean or turkey bacon, I would guess." Norma laughs. "There's no sizzle here. They've taken all the fun out of fatty foods!" Kate sighs.

"We're getting punchy now." Norma smiles broadly. "So this is what having a friend is like."

"What do you mean?" Kate asks. "You were surrounded by people who adored you."

"That's the rub. They adored me. Well, not me, really;

they adored this Marilyn creature." Norma stands a little straighter and runs her hands down her body. "I loved a good time and had some truly great friends, but I kept the hurt deep inside. I discovered that people can't hurt you unless you really let them in."

Kate interjects, "Right. But they can't help you either, unless you let them in."

Norma's face softens. "Guess I never looked at it that way. You know I haven't felt like Norma Jean Baker since maybe 1950. With *Asphalt Jungle* and *All About Eve*, I guess I really became Marilyn Monroe." Kate bunches up her pillow to sit up straighter. She's paying close attention. "Oh, who was that tall British actor in *All About Eve*? He was married to Zsa Zsa."

"That was George Sanders, and he was married to Zsa Zsa and then to Zsa Zsa and Eva's sister, Magda!" Norma replies.

"Talk about keeping it in the family," Kate adds.

Norma laughs. "Right! His new sister-in-law would have also been his ex-wife."

Kate adds, "But he would have had the same mother-in-law!"

Kate looks dreamily at Norma. "I sound like Beth with all my questions, but was it wonderful working with legendary actors like Bette Davis and Sir Laurence Olivier? Must've been intimidating working with actors of their caliber. What was it like?"

Norma smiles. "Like I had died and gone to heaven." She smiles wider. "Well, what I thought heaven might've been like." Norma pauses. She's deep in thought. "Kate, do you think we could've been friends?"

"Want the truth?" Kate asks. Norma nods gently. Kate continues, "I would've liked you, sure. But your fame would've been pretty intimidating. I'm just plain Kate with a husband, kids and a mortgage that would choke a rhino." Norma stands and straightens the bedding. "And a doctor just outside the door." Kate rubs her face. "Great! Bet I look terrific after laughing and crying all morning."

An older doctor in the traditional white lab coat enters the room and looks around to see if Kate is speaking to him. He states, "More laughing than crying, I hope." He takes a seat. "I'm Doctor Cargyle. Want to talk about it, Mrs. Davis?"

Norma knocks her head against the bathroom door. "He's a psychiatrist! Get rid of him, fast! I spent my last lifetime surrounded by shrinks."

Kate is demure. "Really nothing to talk about, Doctor, except that I've been on kind of an emotional roller coaster. I'm just so thankful that my injuries were slight and that I'll be going home soon."

Norma strikes a dramatic pose against the bathroom door, the back of her hand to her brow. "And I'm supposed to be the actress!" She adds in a southern drawl, "Why, doctah, I must look a fright, what with all this laughin' and cryin' I've been doin' all mornin' long."

The doctor closes Kate's chart, then pats her hand. "Well then, Mrs. Davis, I'll let you get ready to go home today." The doctor leaves and Norma takes a small rolling suitcase out of the closet. "Let's pick up your Oscar and then get this show on the road."

Ray loads plants, flowers and balloons on a double-decker rolling hospital cart as Kate sits in her wheelchair. She balked at the ride downstairs but the hospital rules insist that the patient leave the premises firmly planted in a wheelchair. Blaire and Brady, again in their photo-ready, Sunday best outfits, grab their Beanie Babies and drop them on Kate's lap for safekeeping. Ray looks under the bed. "Nope. No pods, but you must be an impostor," he says as he moves in close to get a good look at Kate. "If you truly were my wife, you'd be dreading going home to the white sheets that are now pink because a red Elmo doll was washed with them, and our empty refrigerator; well, empty except for that greenish-brownish lumpy thing in the CorningWare dish, and kids' rooms that look like a cyclone has hit."

Kate throws her head back, "Full speed ahead! It sounds great to me."

A female aide enters the room and pushes Kate's wheelchair through the door as Ray holds it open. "Lead the way," Ray says. Kate looks over her shoulder at Norma. "Coming?" Norma hops up on top of the cart that Ray is pushing. "Wouldn't miss it for the world."

Ray, too, answers Kate, "Of course. I'm right behind you, honey." Ray follows, escorting the kids and pushing the cart with Norma sitting on it. Norma hums *Moonlight Sonata*. Kate snaps her head back at Norma and smiles. She hums *Moonlight Sonata*. Brady says, "Mommy's favorite song."

In the hallways, Norma closely watches people as they pass. While waiting for the elevator, she stares intently at a man's large mobile phone and then reads an advertisement on the back of a boy's shirt for Paul & Del's Frozen Yogurt Shoppe. Norma grimaces. "Frozen yogurt. Yucch!"

Kate shouts back, "I love frozen yogurt."

Ray responds, "I know you do, honey, and I'll get you all

the frozen yogurt you can eat as soon as I get you home and settled." He winks at the aide, leans toward her and whispers, "She's pregnant, you know."

The elevator door opens and a teenage girl with punk magenta hair exits. She's wearing sloppy jeans and a tight black T-shirt with a picture of the Andy Warhol silkscreen of Marilyn Monroe on the front.

Norma inspects the girl's spiky hair, then looks closely at the Marilyn shirt. "Hmmm. Pretty good likeness. But why me? Why not Madame Curie or Golda Meir, women who made a real contribution?"

Kate answers, "You did make a contribution."

"I sure did," Ray says, "Even with decent insurance, it still cost us."

Norma says, "This is getting confusing" and then makes a motion of zipping her lip.

Outside the hospital the aide steers Kate's wheelchair out of the noonday sun, and waits in the shade of a portico as Norma reclines on the nearby loaded cart. Ray pulls up in a maroon minivan and the kids wave wildly from their car seats. Ray pops open the trunk and loads Kate's suitcase and plants. He runs around and opens the passenger door and helps Kate from the wheelchair into the van. Norma says excitedly, "Exterior, Hospital Portico. Noon. The Davis family loads up for the trip home." Norma "pops" through the side of the van into the middle seat. Ray walks around to the driver's side.

Norma says, "Let the adventure begin."

Chapter Six

Quite a Welcome

Ray's van weaves through traffic on a busy freeway, then maneuvers through a maze of side streets. The van enters a manicured subdivision with lovely large homes of fieldstone and brick and spacious, beautifully landscaped yards. Even in the heat of summer, chemically-treated neighborhood lawns are lush and green. Luxury cars are tucked neatly into organized three-car garages. Upscale lawn gym sets and fences are wood or wrought iron, considerably more substantial than in nearby neighborhoods.

The minivan pulls into a quiet cul-de-sac and parks in the circular drive in front of a two-story stone and stucco Tudor home. The large home looks more like an oversized cottage due to the clinging ivy that reaches the second story windows. There are tricycles parked in the shaped shrubbery— a telltale sign that there are children in the household. Draped over this elegant home's front door is Ray's handiwork: a banner taped together from pieces of colored construction paper, announcing in large, colorful letters,

WE ♥ MOMMY

Ray gets out of the van and walks around to get the kids out of their car seats. Beth, in gray silk, stands at the open doorway. She runs to help Kate out of the van. While Ray is removing items from the back, Beth looks around inside the van. She doesn't see Norma sitting right in front of her. Beth whispers to Kate, "Where's your new friend?" Kate says, "She thought it might be best to keep a low profile for a while."

Everyone is settled in Kate's family room. This was the room that had resonated for Kate three years ago during their marathon pre-twins house hunt. They knew they would be having twins and wanted to be settled before the twins arrived. Ray was leaning toward the mid-century house that was tucked precariously into the hills and Kate remembers liking several features of that particular home, one house in the blur of the twelve they visited. She loved the retro black and white tile kitchen floor and the glass blocks next to the vanity in the master bath. The winding garden trail out back had almost sealed the deal, but Kate kept coming back to this house, the one with the bright and airy family room with high ceilings and a look of lived-in elegance. No sooner had they closed escrow than Kate was knee deep in gallons of Navajo Gold and Burnt Umber paint for the family room's burnished walls to make the room even more warm and inviting.

Framed photographs and books now line the stained built-in bookshelves on either side of the beautifully constructed stone fireplace. A smaller "Welcome Home" banner hangs across the fireplace.

Kate's cards and plants line the curved bronze and black-flecked granite counter between the kitchen and family room. The kitchen is big and open with rich terracotta tiles on the floor. The backsplash is an interesting combination of glass mosaic tiles in earth tone shades. There are gleaming white glass-front cabinets and copper pots hanging from a polished copper rack. Coupons and a zillion photos on the large side-by-side refrigerator are held in place by huge pizza slice and chocolate chip cookie magnets.

In the family room Kate lies on the oversized coppery brown leather couch. She snuggles under a chenille throw. There's a piece of chocolate cake on the glass table in front of her. Norma, in her *Gentlemen Prefer Blondes* deep rose-colored gown with a glittery asymmetrical strap across her throat, inspects the bookcase photographs as Brady careens around the corner, picks up a Buzz Lightyear doll, and races out. Beth's two daughters sit on the floor with Blaire, playing with a Furby and assorted Barbie dolls on a geometric print wool rug in just the right shades of gold and copper.

Beth enters the room with her husband, Drew. He's a very attractive gentleman in his mid-forties who resembles ABC News Correspondent Anderson Cooper. He's immaculately attired in a blue oxford cloth shirt, suspenders and glen plaid slacks. His deep tan shows off his silvery close-cropped hair and electric blue eyes. Norma gives Beth the OK sign. Drew meets with her approval.

Drew leans down to Kate and gives her an air kiss. "Accepting visitors?"

Kate reaches up and snaps Drew's suspenders. "Of course, and aren't you a vision as usual." Drew straightens and looks toward Beth. "The Missus insists on perfection," he says. Beth rolls her eyes.

Ray enters the kitchen, then brings a tray with a stainless carafe of coffee and large colorful mugs into the family room and offers a cup to Kate. "The service has certainly improved since my last visit," Kate says. "Guess you had to fire that shrew named Kate who waited on me during my last visit." Ray smiles. "Wish I could think of a great comeback about Kate and *The Taming of the Shrew*, but I'm just about serving the coffee right now."

Drew looks at his watch. Ray asks, "Do you have time to check stock prices on the web?"

"You're on, but my meeting's at two," Drew answers. Drew and Ray exit the family room. Drew comes back through the kitchen. "Glad you're okay, Kate."

Kate answers, "Thanks, Drew."

Kate is still curled up on the couch. Her eyes are closed. Norma sits at the end of the couch. She stares at a *TV Guide* sitting on the table in front of her. The July 31, 1999 cover is a picture of John Kennedy, Jr.

Ray enters the family room. "I'm running the kids over to Rusty's house, honey. Do you need anything?" Kate shakes her head. "No, thanks. I have a remote control and chocolate cake. What more could I need? Is Beth still here?"

Ray answers, "No. She and Drew left a few hours ago." Ray goes to the kitchen and brings the cordless phone to Kate. "Your Mother calls every hour on the hour so she's due again at seven. That's in about ten minutes. Tell her you're turning in early, doctor's orders. I'll be back long before her next call at eight and I can tell her details then." Kate asks, "What details? That I've slept the entire afternoon away?"

Blaire and Brady enter in a rush. Blaire drops her small red "Goin' to Grandma's" suitcase and Brady his camouflage duffel bag. They run to Kate, kissing her and telling her goodnight. Ray asks, "Kate, wouldn't you be more comfortable upstairs?"

Kate settles in further. "No, we'll be fine right here."

"We? Who's we?" Ray inquires. "Gotta mouse in your pocket?"

Kate feels her hip. "Don't think so," she replies. "But what I do have is apparently sleeping sickness. Can't seem to stay awake for more than twenty minutes." Ray answers, "That's good for you. You need the rest."

The doorbell rings. Ray goes to the door. Kate shouts, "Whoever it is, tell 'em I'm still in the hospital." Beth enters, carrying a platter of brownies and a canvas tote bag. Her teal, lace-edged Capris match the teal in her abstract floral top. "That flimsy excuse won't work with me. I know better," she says.

Ray leans into the room and apologizes, "Sorry, she broke through the barricade." He turns his attention to the kids. "No chocolate, kids. I just got your faces clean. Come on, let's get going." The kids and Ray leave the room and shout their good-byes as Kate reaches for a brownie.

Beth looks from the piece of chocolate cake to the brownie in Kate's hand. "Chocolate cake *and* a brownie. What's the matter, Katie-Boo, eating for two?"

Kate glares. "We've sworn off baby talk until tomorrow."

Beth responds matter-of-factly, "Can't keep your head in the fucking sand forever." Kate responds, "Maybe not forever but no baby talk at least until tomorrow."

Beth crouches down to look under the end table. "Come out, come out, wherever you are."

Norma stands up from the couch and spins. She manifests herself directly in front of Beth. She leans over to make eye contact. Beth looks up at Norma's cleavage bursting from the white *Seven Year Itch* dress.

Beth smiles. "Welcome back!" She stands and unceremoniously dumps books and tabloids from her tote bag and sprays them on the cocktail table in front of the couch. Marilyn Monroe is on all the covers.

Kate sits up and picks through the books. "Where'd you get all these?"

Beth responds, "My slutty neighbor, you know, Rebecca, the divorced nurse practitioner with the devil worshiper son, is this monster Marilyn fan, so I borrowed these for my sick friend." Norma sorts through the pile of books and tabloids and picks up a book: *Marilyn, My Wife For Life*, by Joel Tremont. She's incredulous. "I don't remember ever being married to a guy named Joel."

Beth scowls. "Lyin' pricks, hounding you to death after you're dead. You probably met him one time at a party or something, but that wouldn't make much of a book, so he sold someone a crock that he was married to you."

Kate says, "Terry Moore said she was married to Howard Hughes. She got a piece of his estate."

Beth laughs. "Guess I could someday say that Bill Gates and I ran off and eloped and never had it annulled. I'd be happy with a slice of that dough."

Kate says, "Oh, and what about Elvis!"

Beth replies, "Guess I could've been married to Elvis, too!"

Norma says, "What a sweet man, and he's sure crazy about Lisa Marie." Norma adds wistfully, "I knew him in life, too. Well, momentarily!" The ladies laugh.

Kate explains, "I mean the Elvis sightings that went on for years after his death. Like he'd really be salting the fries at

Burger King."

Beth interjects, "They won't let the poor pudgy greaser rest in peace." Before anyone can comment, Beth adds, "Speaking of which, Norma, how come you're not resting in peace?"

Kate clears her throat, hoping to distract Beth. It's about as successful as talking about going home and watching TV would be in stopping a willful child from crying for Tic Tacs or bubblegum at the Kmart checkout. Kate takes another stab at changing the subject. She points at a picture in one of the books. "Take a look at this bathroom, Beth. Hot-and-cold running luxury."

Beth actually does veer from her question for a brief moment to glance at the photo. "Whoa. A lady could do some serious damage in a tub like that." She then turns immediately to Norma and asks again, "Have you been restless, Norma, since you died?"

Since the diversion didn't work, Kate tries once again to mercifully change the subject. "Did you love living in luxury, Norma?"

Norma glances at the book and the picture. "It was nice, sure, but all I really ever wanted..." she trails off and waves her hand around the room, then continues, "was this, the house in the suburbs, a husband..."

Beth interrupts, "Preferably a husband who can sustain a hard-on for more than eleven seconds."

Norma shakes her head at Beth.

Wistfully, Norma almost whispers, "And a baby or two. But it just wasn't meant to be."

Norma flips through the stack of magazines and books. She glances through a hardback book and stops at a grainy black and white photo of Marilyn Monroe, face down on the bed with a sheet hastily thrown across her nude body. Her outstretched arm dangles from the bed...inches away from the phone receiver that lies on the carpet. Policemen mill about the room in the photograph that is splashed across the front page of a newspaper dated August 5, 1962 with a glaring headline:

MARILYN MONROE FOUND DEAD IN BED, NUDE

Norma envisions that fateful day almost thirty-seven years ago. She lies face down, completely nude on the bed in her darkened bedroom. She runs her hand through her hair as she speaks into the phone, slurring her words. "Uh huh, hmm. I understand." Then she drops her head. "I did call but he never called me back. Tell him I love him." Her arm drops off the side of the bed. The phone receiver falls. Her phone continually buzzes.

A large, glowing sunburst, radiating golden rays of light, travels from Marilyn's lifeless body up to and through the heavily-draped window.

Outside in the dark of night, behind the large sunburst a pulsating smaller sunburst floats up through the clouds. They stop floating and hover only a second before Peg, in her hooded gown, takes the ever-present pencil from her hood and approaches the sunbursts. "Marilyn Monroe and Boy Monroe, I'm Peg and I'll escort you through Processing. I know you'll have a lot of questions and I'm here to help you both make the transition." The larger sunburst is now a gauzy spirit with Marilyn's features. Spirit Marilyn looks totally disoriented and confused. "Boymonroe? Who's Boymonroe?" Peg double-checks her records and responds, "It's right here on my checklist, Boy Monroe. Your son."

Spirit Marilyn immediately spins away from the small sunburst. Marilyn insists, "You must be mistaken. I don't have a son." Peg lightly blows the small sunburst into Norma. She checks her records yet again. "Your *unborn* son."

Marilyn laments, "Why now? When it's too late?"

"It's not too late for him," Peg states. "There's a birth scheduled in fourteen seconds in Louisville, Kentucky; a seven pound, four ounce brunette girl will be born to first time parents. She'll be called Kathryn Loyal Malone." Norma whirls around the smaller sunburst as Peg continues, "Or we have blonde Jeremy Benson Foster, an eight pound, seven ounce boy to be born in Toledo in fifteen seconds. He'll be the third child, with an older sister and brother."

Norma is spinning. "It's all too much. I'm ashamed to say that I'm not even sure who his father is. Oh, do I have to give him up so soon?"

Peg answers matter-of-factly, "Afraid so. Unborns go again right away. As for shame, it's wasted energy. Let it go."

The Norma spirit morphs again into a large sunburst that grows even larger and brighter in intensity. Norma's soft voice questions Peg, "Anything I should do?"

Peg replies, "Just send along your love for your baby's journey home. It's an act of great unselfishness."

The larger sunburst whirls around the smaller one in a silent dance. For moments they meld as one, sending off sparks in a kaleidoscope of color and light. Then the smaller sunburst, now glowing with brighter intensity leaps outside the gale force winds. Momentarily, the smaller sunburst becomes a spirit entity and Marilyn gets a glimpse of a tow-headed infant boy. He has piercing blue eyes and soft dimpled cheeks.

Spirit Marilyn whispers, "The thing I wanted more than anything else—a child.

Peg encourages from the sidelines, "Better hurry. Will it be Kate in Louisville or Jeremy in Toledo?"

"Good-bye, my son. I wish you much love. Enjoy your life as Kate," Marilyn says.

The smaller sunburst darts away.

The large sunburst flickers, then dims.

The sound of muffled sobs fills the night sky.

In Kate's family room, Beth loudly clears her throat to snap Norma out of her trance-like state.

Norma shakes her head to loosen the cobwebs. The Marilyn Monroe books and tabloids are still strewn across the cocktail table. Kate leans in close to Norma, "Welcome back, Norma."

Beth agrees, "Yeah. You were a zillion miles away. Now tell us, Norma, how come you're still churning in heaven?"

Norma responds, "Unresolved issues."

Beth questions further. "Don't you want to just settle down and enjoy it?"

Kate puts her hand over Beth's mouth. "Sorry about Beth, Norma. She sometimes gets carried away, but she means well." Beth tries to talk but acts like she can't because of Kate's hand. The ladies all laugh.

Chapter Seven

South of the Border

Kate is sound asleep on the family room couch as Norma stands at the bookshelves, examining book titles and baby photos. She's in the short, low-cut, black nightie from *Some Like It Hot*. Ray enters the room and adjusts Kate's cover. He asks gently, "Coming upstairs?" In response, Kate only pulls the cover in closer. Ray leans down and gently kisses her. She halfheartedly kisses air and slurs, "Love you." Ray answers, "Love you, too, baby." He turns off the family room lamps and leaves the room. He goes into the kitchen and loads a few saucers into the dishwasher. "Can't tell you," Ray says, "how empty this house seemed without you." Kate mumbles, "Thanks." Ray then goes upstairs, leaving on the kitchen overhead light.

Norma wistfully runs a finger over a silver-framed Christmas picture of the newborn twins, then one in a pewter frame of the twins together at the beach.

Norma then goes to the window. In the dark sky, one star shines brighter than the others, twinkling for attention. "Very soon, Peg," Norma says telepathically. "I think I'm going to tell her about my son, but it's still so weird. I carried a blonde son and she's a dark-haired, soon-to-be-thirty-seven-year-old woman, but Kate has exactly the qualities I would've wanted in my own child."

Peg responds by blinking, then Norma continues. "No, I know she's not my child. She'll never be my child. She's very much Paul and Kay Malone's daughter, but I can rest now." There's a slight pause and then Norma says softly, "Peg, I would've wanted my son to be a grounded, secure, compassionate person, just like Kate. I really would've wanted that for him. Kate's loving nature makes me just as happy and proud as if I had seen those qualities in my own son."

Norma pauses again wistfully for a moment, as though taking one last backward look, then brightens. "No more being sad about the life I could have had but didn't. I'm not sure how much I'll tell Kate, but I'm going to enjoy being with her until I return to my...day job. There's a lot to be said for resting in peace."

Peg blinks. Norma smiles. "I agree, Peg. 'Way to go, Norma Jean!'"

Norma turns and joins Kate on the couch. Kate stirs, rubs her face briskly and strains to see her watch. "Two a.m.?" she questions. "I've slept the whole night away." Kate picks up the phone and shakes it slightly. "You mean the phone didn't ring all night long?"

Norma points her index finger toward the cordless phone base on the kitchen counter. As Norma points, there's a beeping sound from the kitchen. The light goes on and off on the base of the kitchen phone. Kate laughs and shoves Norma slightly, "You put the phone out of commission?" Norma points her finger toward the TV. It goes on. She shakes her finger at it, as if correcting a bad child. The TV flips channels at a furious pace. Norma shakes her head in disbelief. "Too many choices," she says, but then pauses as the TV screen captures an energetic young couple going at it against a small bathroom wall. He's pumping away as she moans and groans dramatically. Norma continues, "Although this looks promising."

Kate playfully grabs Norma's finger and shakes it at the TV. Channels again fly by in feverish clips of commercials, runway shows, infomercials, news and reruns. Kate points Norma's finger directly at the screen. The TV goes dark. Both women settle back on the couch. Norma picks up a black shadowbox-framed photograph from the side table and looks at the darling baby captured in the picture. It's hard to tell if the baby's Brady or Blaire.

Kate says, "Brady at eight weeks. He was a real beauty."

Norma sighs, "I had a son once, but I had to give him up. It was August 5th..."

Before Norma can complete her thought, Kate runs her hand lightly over Norma's. Still half-asleep, Kate slurs, "That's my birthday!" Norma squeezes Kate's hand. "I know, it's almost your birthday." Kate sits up slightly. "Your miscarriages must have been devastating." Norma clutches Kate's hand with an even tighter grip. Kate says, "Having children was the single most eventful moment of my life. Not that I'm necessarily ready for another one."

Norma says wistfully, "Children are a real privilege."

Kate strokes the picture. "Guess it must seem to you like the world's forgetting that." Moments pass in the quiet, then Kate continues, "Can you see what's going on down here on earth? Or is it even really down?"

"Not really up or down, more all-around, sort of eye-level," Norma responds. "At first you look back a lot, then less and less as time passes. You naturally want so much to help your loved ones back on earth, but all you can do is help present opportunities, and it's up to them to take advantage or not."

"Like?" Kate questions.

"Like little clues that may lead to a conclusion. If you're weighing say two job opportunities, one in Phoenix and one in Denver, you may begin seeing all kinds of news reports about Phoenix. That's just a little nudge that may lead you in the right direction or at least get you to stop and listen for a moment. The key is to listen. If you keep hearing evidence from your friends that the guy you're with is wrong for you, then you need to pay attention. The key is to listen."

Norma pauses for a moment, then continues, "I wish I could've done a more convincing job of sending down messages to help avoid the night at the L.A. Ambassador Hotel or the grassy knoll at Dealey Plaza in Dallas or..." Kate interrupts, "You do the best you can!" Norma continues, "But I've observed a lot more lately since I knew that I would be accompanying you back. And I do agree. There's some pretty weird stuff going on here on earth."

Kate pulls the cover over her face. "Is there ever! But that's no reason for me to have considered abandoning my family. Norma, I wanted to stay with Nanny and never look back. I'm so ashamed. My first priority should have been to get back here and be with Ray and the kids." Norma pulls the cover away from Kate's face. "As a wise woman once told me, shame is wasted energy. Let it go." Kate is soothed.

They sit for a few minutes without speaking. Norma says gently, "That's the way you're supposed to feel when you're in the kingdom. You don't feel responsibility, so you can begin learning. It's all about learning, to be better, more complete. Kate, all your senses were overwhelmed. Who wouldn't want to stay in that peaceful, warm, loving environment? You can't blame yourself."

Kate nods. "That makes me feel better. I thought it made me a lousy mother if I hadn't thought first of my responsibility to the kids." Kate yawns. Norma says, "You couldn't be a lousy mother if you tried."

Kate replies, "You're pretty maternal yourself, Norma Jean. You have great instincts."

Norma smiles. "For the first time I'm actually feeling close to what a mother must feel when her child is upset or hurt or just needs to be consoled."

Kate yawns again. "Sorry, can we pick this up again tomorrow?" Kate collapses back on the couch. Norma says, "Sure. We have plenty of time." Norma covers Kate and gently runs her hands through Kate's hair. "That's a promise," Norma says.

Early Wednesday morning, Kate fusses around the kitchen in her striped seersucker robe and listens on the cordless phone. She occasionally grunts as a response but there's no real conversation on her part. Blaire and Brady sit on stools at the counter in their pajamas, eating cereal and staring at cereal boxes. Norma, way overdressed in the sequined "Happy Birthday, Mr. President" dress, leans against the counter from the kitchen side and reads aloud from the back of Brady's cereal box: "Follow the path to hidden treasures for Jimmy Giraffe and his safari crew." Then she leans over to read the side panel: "Sugar, corn meal, cocoa, canola and/or rice bran oil, corn syrup, corn starch, modified corn starch."

Kate finally speaks into the phone. "Mom, there's no need to make the trip. Really. I'm fine. Yes, I'll call you later today. I love you too." Kate clicks the phone off and it immediately rings again. Kate answers. "Hey, Beth. No, the kids are here. They both came home instead. They were going to spend the night at Rusty's, but they wanted to be with their Mom." There's a long pause. "Sure, I'd love to get out of the house and go shopping." Another pause. "Okay, I'll see you in about an hour." Kate hangs up the phone. She points toward Norma, then toward the phone, then drops her head like she's dead. Norma points toward the phone and shakes her finger. The phone is now out of commission.

Kate gathers cereal boxes and puts them away in a large pantry. Brady objects, "Mommy!" Kate replies, "I hate to interrupt when you're reading the classics, but it's almost time to leave. You know that your Dad will be pulling out of the drive right at eight twenty-five and that's in three minutes." Kate holds up three fingers.

The kids jump down and run out of the room as Ray enters. He adjusts his blue and gray striped tie that looks great with his blue shirt that has tiny gray checks and his steel gray suit.

"See! What did I tell you?" Kate asks. "You have three minutes."

Ray takes his coffee mug to the sink. As he passes he pats Kate's rear end and nuzzles her neck. "Don't overdo it today." Ray grabs the newspaper off the counter, folds it and places it in his attaché case that sits open on the built-in desk.

In two and a half minutes the kids rush back into the room. Brady has on *Toy Story* swim trunks and carries a beach towel and a small red vinyl bag. Blaire wears a neon orange

Little Kitty one-piece swimsuit and carries a small flowered tote bag. Ray says, "Don't worry, Kate. I've made all the arrangements. Rusty's Mom offered to keep the kids today after swimming lessons. They have a change of clothes in their bag and I'll swing by to pick them up on my way home so you can enjoy your day." Kate smiles. "I'm impressed, Mister Mom!" Ray and the kids exit the kitchen to the garage, blowing kisses and shouting good-byes.

Norma says, "There's sure a lot of love in this house." Kate smiles proudly. She motions for Norma to follow her. They walk to the two-story entry foyer that has a variegated slate floor, high arched palladium windows and long rectangular leaded glass panels on either side of the heavy, ornate door. A carved table and antique claw-foot chair sit at the base of the curved stairwell. A large vase filled with flowers left over from the hospital visit sits in the center of the table.

Kate opens the heavy front door and waves wildly just as Ray pulls in front of the house and stops. The kids yell out the window, "Dance, Mommy."

Kate steps out on the front porch and raises her arms over her head and does an exaggerated ballerina pirouette. The kids cheer her on from the car. Kate blows them kisses, and then waves madly as the car pulls away and heads out of the cul-de-sac.

Kate goes back into the house and closes the door. She joins Norma in the seldom-used, beautifully decorated living room. The walls are a deep taupe. The detailed crown molding is stark white, as is the window trim. The billowing floral fabric in muted shades of olive, gold and rust is draped across the large windows with a coordinating striped scarf draped across the top. The drapes fall into graceful puddles on the polished hardwood floors in deep mahogany.

They take a seat on the ivory brocade couch. Kate clutches the tapestry pillows close to her chest and again fights off tears. "To think I could've lost them." Norma runs her hand along Kate's arm. "I know. You're here one day and then poof! It's all over. Sure makes you think." Kate leans her head on Norma's shoulder. Norma says dreamily, "To treasure each moment. You need to give your husband and kids a special hug because you truly never know which moment will be your last."

Kate comes into the kitchen. She's wearing biker shorts and a long gray Nike "Just Do It" T-shirt. "I refuse to sleep the day away again." She shakes her arms around. "Let's get moving." Norma follows Kate in the kitchen as Kate runs a sponge across the counter. Norma leans against the bar stool because she has trouble sitting in the tight-fitting gown. Kate picks up Ray's coffee mug and holds it a second before putting it in the dishwasher.

Norma says, "Ray's sure a gem. Where'd you find him?" Kate smiles. "Actually he found me. I was lost and he gave me directions. I mean literally. I was searching for the bar exam room and he helped me find my way there. He's been helping me find my way ever since."

Kate again flaps her arms wildly. "Too much inactivity. I'm getting so stiff. Up for some marathon shopping?" Norma nods. "I'll be glad to tag along. Afraid I was never much of a shopper." Kate laughs. "Oh, don't worry. Beth will have you converted to the Church of Everlasting Bargains before lunch."

Norma agrees. "Beth is quite a character."

Kate laughs. "She isn't as hard-shell as she tries to appear. I've seen her cry during commercials for long distance phone service. She also actually covers up those coordinated designer outfits with a plain canvas apron when she works at the Conner Street Shelter." Kate smiles. "She's good-hearted, just confused."

Norma asks, "Have you been friends a long time?" Kate answers, "Not really, just a few years. It just seems like a long time!" The women laugh.

The ladies load into Beth's beige Volvo wagon that's parked out front in Kate's circular drive. Kate gets in the front seat, Norma in the back. Beth eyes Norma's dress, then pulls at her own orange sherbet silk tank top. "I'm way underdressed. Is there a premiere at J.C. Penney's today?" Kate immediately answers, "You go with what you know." Beth sings in a wispy, breathless voice, "Happy Birthday, Mister President."

They drive past well-dressed young mothers with their well-dressed toddlers and fashionably small dogs. Norma says, "This is a lovely neighborhood." Beth turns to ask, "Norma, how long do you think the Davises will stay in this nice neighborhood if Kate gives up corporate law?" Kate counters, "I was drawn to the law, not the boardroom. I want to make a difference."

Beth shakes her head. "You'll make a difference all right, a big difference right in the paycheck. And bye-bye to quarterly bonus checks." Kate puts her hand on Beth's shoulder. "You're on vacation and I'm on short term disability. Let's forget the office." Beth drums the steering wheel. "Forget the office, forget the baby. Seems everything's off limits." Kate glares at Beth.

Kate thinks for a moment and then says, "Maybe Public Defender. There's got to be more satisfaction in the law somewhere outside the boardroom."

Beth insists, "All I'm saying is satisfaction is a little overrated if you have to kiss those fucking-A stock options good-bye." Kate beams. "And good-bye to cold, heartless law."

Beth weaves through traffic, trying to remove the plastic strip from a CD as she drives. "Anybody carrying a Black and Decker saw? These fucking plastic strips!" Beth pops the plastic strip and her nail with it. She puts the CD in the player. Soon Elton John is singing "Candle in the Wind." Kate turns to Norma, "This is a lovely tribute to you, Norma. It's by Elton John. He and Bernie Taupin wrote it about ten years after you died. Start it over, Beth."

"Candle in the Wind"

> Though I never knew you at all
> You had the grace to hold yourself
> While those around you crawled
> They crawled out of the woodwork
> And they whispered into your brain
> They set you on a treadmill
> And they made you change your name
>
> And it seems to me you lived your life
> Like a candle in the wind
> Never knowing who to cling to
> When the rain set in

Beth drives in silence, the emotion in Elton John's voice saying it all. Norma wipes a tear from her face. "My God! That's beautiful."

They pull into the mall parking lot. Beth circles and

circles until she spots a woman in the front row loading her trunk with packages. Beth pulls up and stops. The woman gets in her car...and sits. Beth leans out the window and shouts, "What're you doing, balancing your checkbook?" Beth honks the horn. The woman flips her off, but starts her car and pulls out of the space.

Kate, Norma and Beth rubberneck down the main walkway. They are a peculiar trio: Norma in sequins, Kate in her casual Nike attire, and Beth in ice cream colored silk tank top and shorts. Norma stares at a window display featuring a live mannequin modeling a revealing bikini. "And they said I was provocative!" Beth stands back to get the full view of Norma in her skintight dress. "How dare they! I can barely see your nips through the sequins." Beth slowly moves on as Kate and Norma stare at the bikini. Kate says to Norma, "Ray would never let Blaire wear something like that, well, until she's well into her thirties." Two teenage boys pass by. The taller of the two boys holds a skateboard; the other holds a giant Icee drink. They laugh at Kate talking to herself. One boy says to the other, "She's probably high on something."

Beth stops at the next store to admire a masculine display. The chiseled male mannequin is in a luxurious burgundy fleur-de-lis printed silk robe and boxers. Beth says, "Drew thinks silk boxers are wimpy. Mister Limp Dick worries about what's manly." Norma lingers at the display. "I always liked men, really liked them. There's something comforting about their self-assuredness." Beth adds, "No wonder they're self-assured. Testosterone and a fucking collegiate tie will get you anything on the menu." Beth stops and sniffs loudly. "Speaking of menus, I'm never wrong! It's Beef Broccoli day at Chop Sticks and it's noon already."

The ladies enter the mall food court. Small restaurants surround them. Norma excitedly looks around at the selection. "Oh! Yo Quiero Taco Bell, the run for the border place!" She spins around, "Ooh! And Quarter Pounder!"

Beth interjects, "Been watching a little TV since you've been here, Norma?"

Kate laughs. "The funniest part is that Norma doesn't eat or drink."

Norma says, "I just love all the choices."

As Norma spins to get the whole panoramic effect, her sequins glisten. "A Whopper!" Beth covers Norma's mouth. Her outstretched arm now dangles in midair. The boys who passed them upstairs are seated across the food court. They nudge each other and laugh.

In the mall walkway, Beth and Kate try on sunglasses at a center aisle kiosk. Kate, in oversized Jackie O sunglasses, turns to Norma. "Do I look like a movie star?" Norma answers, "No, more like a real person. That's even better."

The ladies walk on, ducking into a record store. Kate and Beth look through CDs as Norma closely, very closely, inspects life-sized cutouts of Michael Bolton and Steven Tyler of Aerosmith.

Early that evening, Kate sits on the edge of the four-poster bed in their huge master bedroom. Rich fabrics in shades of burgundy, olive and sage green are on the bed and at the large windows. Antique quilts are stacked in an open distressed white French country corner hutch. The massive armoire with baskets of ivy spilling over the top fills the side focus wall that has been painted a deep burgundy. A small portable TV rests on the triple dresser. Ray paces the room.

"It's your decision, Kate."

Kate sighs. "I just can't imagine having another baby." Ray leans over Kate to rub her shoulders, then leans her back on the bed and lightly runs his finger down her throat to the top button of her blouse. "And I was excited at the prospect of those humongous..."

There's a loud and persistent knock on the bedroom door. Brady says, "Hungry, Mommy." Kate smoothes her shirt, stands and walks to the bedroom door, turning back to Ray. Before she can say anything, Brady adds, "Bacaroni and cheese."

Kate and Brady enter the kitchen. Brady heads down to the family room and the toy chest while Kate gets busy in the kitchen. Norma sits on the family room floor next to Blaire and her Legos. Norma slowly gathers all the blue ones together. Blaire is confused. She looks at the neat bundle of blue Legos, then up at her Mom busy in the kitchen. She goes back to her play. Norma glances at Blaire as she concentrates on her building. Blaire screws up her face, her tongue darting around the corners of her mouth for further concentration.

As Norma watches Blaire with her Legos, instead of two-year-old Blaire, Norma sees a statuesque twelve-year-old Blaire, her long auburn hair now deeper brown with reddish highlights and held back off her porcelain face with a headband. Instead of Legos, she's surrounded with schoolbooks. She wears a round-collar white blouse and plaid skirt, reminiscent of those worn as a uniform in parochial schools.

HELLO, NORMA JEAN

Chapter Eight

Visions

The Davis family sits at the massive table in the airy dining room. There's a beautiful arrangement of silk flowers on the antique sideboard. Norma observes the family meal from a side chair. Ray says, "Fancy, huh kids? Eating in the 'birfday' room. We usually have only our holiday and birthday dinners in here. But tomorrow, on August 5th, Mommy will be thirty-seven." Kate holds a spoonful of macaroni, ready to launch at Ray. Ray plays like he's ducking to dodge the oncoming food.

Kate laughs. "Never mind. It would probably hit Brady anyway. He usually wears his food." They look at Brady. He has a green bean on his cheek and macaroni and cheese around his mouth.

Just like Blaire with her schoolbooks, Norma envisions a future date where the two-year-old Brady sitting at the dining room table is now a strapping twelve-year-old. He bites into a hamburger, leaving a trail of ketchup smeared across his face. He wears braces and has an open, friendly face that is framed with dark auburn curls.

Norma takes a deep breath. Brady is once again the macaroni-smeared two-year-old. Norma looks at Ray, who sits at the head of the table. Slowly, Ray fades and then disappears from view. His place at the table is empty.

Norma runs from the dining room.

Kate follows. Ray looks up as Kate leaves the room. Ray says, "Need anything? I'll get it." Kate answers, "Thanks. I'll be right back. I think I left the oven on."

In Kate's family room, Kate joins Norma at the window. "Are you okay?" Norma responds, "I'm fine. The emotion just took me by surprise. You'd better get back to your family." Norma whimpers softly. Kate comforts her.

In the fish-theme bathroom that is positioned between Blaire's and Brady's bedrooms, the twins splash in the tub as Kate kneels on the fish-shaped floor mat and sponges them. Norma's propped up on the toilet. Norma is in the bright pink strapless dress that she has hiked up to make herself comfortable. Blaire moves aside in the tub to allow Brady to scoot over toward Kate. Soapsuds drip from his hair. Kate runs a sponge behind his ears. "Ooh, Mommy's legs don't like this," Kate complains. Blaire replies, "Mommy's three seven. Daddy said so." Kate reaches in and splashes them. "Not yet, you bubbly buzzards. Not quite yet." Kate and Norma laugh as the kids take a good splashing.

Blaire snuggles in her white iron daybed. Barbie dolls surround the bed and printed Barbies are on the bedspread, Roman shades, and pillow shams.

Kate sits on a wicker stool by the bed, Norma on the edge of the bed. Kate whispers, "Daddy will be up in a minute." Kate leans over to kiss Blaire. Blaire first offers the honored Doctor Barbie, who gets to spend the night in the bed. Kate pecks Doctor Barbie's coiffure, then gives Blaire a big hug. Kate straightens and yet Blaire keeps holding on. Kate pries away her arms. Blaire asks, "Much as the sky?"

Kate scoffs, "Of course as much as the sky! Why, I love you as much as Toys 'R Us." Kate kisses Blaire. Contented, Blaire snuggles down in the bed. Kate turns off the overhead light as they leave the room. Blaire's face glows from the pink light of a Barbie-face night light. Norma says, "You've got it all, you lucky lady." Kate answers, "Thanks. I need reminding every once in a while."

Brady's room is strictly Elmo territory: plastic, stuffed, inflatable, wind-up, moveable, bendable, poseable Elmos peek out from every surface. Twin bed Elmo bedspreads and throw pillows complete the theme.

Kate and Norma watch Brady root around in the toy box for his dream companion. The bright green toy box is plastered with Elmo decals. Kate picks up stray clothing and toys. She dangles a stuffed "ticklish" Elmo doll. "Looking for this?" Brady grabs the small stuffed toy and jumps into bed. Kate tucks him in and then sits beside him. Norma sits on the other twin bed. Brady giggles as Kate smothers him with little kisses. He flexes his arm for inspection. Kate hugs him. "Much as the house?" he asks. Kate scoffs, "Of course as much as the house! Why, I love you as much as, as this whole neighborhood." Brady is all smiles. "All the way over to Rusty's house?" Kate replies, "Even further than Rusty's."

Norma smiles. "That's so reassuring. It's so wonderful to love, and to be loved."

Kate walks to the door and turns off the overhead light. Brady and Norma are bathed in the Western Roundup Woody night light, the only piece left of *Toy Story* since Elmo took over the premises. Norma says, "I think I'll stay awhile and watch him sleep."

On the back deck, Ray and Kate sit on side-by-side black wrought iron gliders. Ray's feet are propped up on the low, round glass table. "You know, these moments we have together are so special. I'm so glad to have you back home, and back with us." Ray starts to break down. Kate comforts him, "I know, honey. It makes us realize how much we have to be thankful for, and how lucky we are to have one another, and our kids, and our lives together." Ray wipes his eyes. "I'd just as soon not be tested again anytime soon."

Kate smiles. "I know what you mean."

Norma reclines next to Brady on his twin bed, watching him sleep. She's propped up on one elbow, gently stroking Brady's hair across his forehead. "Wonder how different my life would have been if I had been around to raise my son, if I hadn't been so fragile, so easily wounded." Brady makes a small noise as he exhales. "Sleep, little man. Let your world be filled with Elmo and Buzz Lightyear and hugs and kisses and lots of love."

Ray stands and massages his lower back. "I'm gonna hit the shower. Coming up?" Kate mumbles, "Soon." Ray points to the threatening sky, "Looks like storm clouds are gathering." Kate sits up enough to take notice. "Don't worry. With my new aversion to water, I'll be in at the first drop of rain." Ray goes to the French doors leading to the family room. "Need anything?" Kate answers, "No, thanks. I have everything I need." Ray smiles. She adds, "Really, honey. I'm just fine."

Ray goes into the house. Kate leans her head back and closes her eyes.

About six miles away, Beth and Drew lie on their queen-size bed; each on their own side, as far away from one another as possible; each hugging their edge of the bed, facing out. Beth faces west reading a novel, and Drew faces east, concentrating on the financial pages. Surprisingly—since Beth always coordinates everything—the room is spare, even antiseptic, with very little color, few accessories, and even fewer personal items. It's as if they've gone out of their way not to personalize the bedroom, other than with a few family photos on the dresser. It has never been painted beyond the builder's bland off-white, with a small splash of sea-foam green on the bathroom wall that is visible from the bedroom. Norma, in Sugar's flapper dress from *Some Like It Hot*, "pops" through the back wall of the bathroom.

"Okay, gal," Norma says to herself, "You kissed Tony Curtis, you can surely get through this."

The white marble double vanity is clearly divided in half: Drew's side is populated with Polo cologne, Aquafresh and Zest, Beth's side with Estee Lauder, Crest and Clinique soap. Other than the small sea-foam green embroidered detailing on the hem of the white guest towels that matches the sea-foam wall above the vanity, the bathroom is white on white. Norma fluffs her hair in the mirror and leans out to look back in the bedroom.

Norma observes as Drew reaches up and turns off his small bedside lamp. "Goodnight, Beth," he says softly. Beth answers, "'Night." Drew pushes and punches his pillow.

Norma says to herself, "I'll bet you could get it up, Drew, if you just tried."

Drew, his pillow just right, settles in for sleep. Beth

draws even closer to her edge of the bed and continues reading.

Norma opens the bathroom linen closet: row after row of all white towels and uniform columns of toiletries. She quietly closes the door, then goes to the vanity and dabs on Beth's Estee Lauder Pleasures perfume. Norma opens the walk-in closet doors. The doors squeak slightly. Norma listens for Beth or Drew. There's no response.

Beth's side of the enormous closet is arranged by color, sub-arranged by shade and sub-sub arranged by texture. Shoes are neatly aligned under their respective color group. Drew's side is neat but not obsessive. Norma smiles, then switches half a dozen of Beth's shoes around so the pairs no longer match.

Norma enters the bedroom. Beth has left her light on, but she has fallen asleep holding her book. Norma looks at the small, delicate photos on the dresser, smiling faces of Erin and Meagan, smiling faces of Beth and Drew in happier times. "What happened to those beautiful smiles?" Norma asks. Norma walks to the bed and leans in close to Drew. He smiles broadly and moans, "Mmmm."

"Looks pretty lively to me, Drew. All systems go." Norma gets into bed and backs up against Drew, pulling his arms around her, guiding his caresses. Drew needs little coaxing. His hands glide across Norma's skin. "Like silk," he says dreamily. Drew opens his eyes and turns to look at Beth, sleeping soundly. He looks around the room and then lays back down. He throws his arm over his forehead. Norma grabs Drew's hands and holds them behind his head as she leans into him. Drew turns to Norma, moving to her rhythm. Drew is a bucking bronco with no rider. He jolts upright, knocking

Norma back.

Drew sits on the edge of the bed, turns on his lamp and pulls open his pajama bottoms to check for activity. Pleased, he gets up and walks toward the bathroom. "Fully functional," he says.

Norma jumps out of bed and races to meet Drew at the bathroom door. She pushes against him. Drew takes a deep breath and then runs his hands through his thinning hair. "Goddamn! Don't let this dream end." Drew cautiously steps forward. Norma lifts her dress and puts her foot up on the doorjamb to block him. She pivots her leg and massages him with her knee. Drew runs his hand up Norma's leg. Norma reaches for him. Drew leans his head back and closes his eyes. Norma inquires, "What happened to your spark, Drew? Ready to ignite it?"

Drew can't resist. He backs Norma up against the wall, grabs her and lifts her up to him. Drew opens his eyes. He's pinned flat against the wall. Embarrassed, he abruptly looks toward the bed. Beth is sleeping soundly.

Norma cheers him on. "There you go, Drew baby!"

Drew walks almost to the bed and then quickly turns and enters the bathroom. Norma follows him.

Drew opens the vanity drawer and takes out a few *Playboys*. He grabs the seventy-five dollar *Playboy* from 1953. The cover is Marilyn Monroe as 1953's "Sweetheart of the Month" in *Playboy*'s very first issue.

Drew closes the bathroom door. He says, "Looks like it's not MY problem, Beth."

Norma immediately leaves the bathroom and "pops" through to the bedroom. She leans against the closed bathroom door, defeated. She walks over and gently removes Beth's book from her hands. She lays the book, *Energized Sex*, on the night table. Norma tiptoes back to the bathroom door, then stops to listen. Drew asks, "Can't ever be perfect enough for you, can I, Beth? No wonder I gave up trying." Norma runs her hand against the bathroom door. "Maybe you and Beth can find your smiles again, Drew. I sure hope so."

On Kate's deck, Norma glides on the glider next to a sleeping Kate. The rocker squeaks and Kate opens her eyes. She stretches. "The answer hasn't come to me yet. Think it's selfish of me to want our lives to stay the way they are now?" Norma answers, "Nothing stays the same, Kate. Afraid I can't advise you, as much as I wanted to raise a child." Kate counters, "I also wanted a baby, very much. And then there were two!" Norma takes a deep breath and pats Kate's hand. The wind picks up. Kate holds her hair back out of her face.

Norma continues, "Everything happens for a reason, Kate. I thought I couldn't go on living because the man I loved..."

Kate puts her hand on Norma's chair. It stops rocking. She inquires, "You truly loved him, didn't you?" Norma responds, "More than life itself, but it isn't who you think. It was..."

Kate stops her. "I don't need to know." Kate looks to the darkening sky. "You'll be leaving soon?"

Norma bites her lip. The ladies hold hands as the storm clouds hover. Kate adds, "You're a special person, Norma. Very special."

Norma smiles. "The irony is, I could have saved myself —and those who were closest to me—a lot of pain, if only I'd believed that." The ladies lean back and enjoy the silence.

Norma again envisions a future date. Kate, dressed in black, holds an infant in a small paneled office. Beth enters the office and leans close to whisper something to her. Kate rises and hands the baby to Beth. Kate leaves the room, then walks slowly down a carpeted corridor. She enters a room to her right. On the door is a placard: Ray Davis, funeral services at noon.

Norma shakes her head to clear the vision. The citronella candle next to Kate flickers in the breeze. She looks to Norma. "You'll be leaving soon, won't you?" Norma nods and then says softly, "I have a little while yet." The candle is blown out. Their only light is from the next door neighbor's floodlight. Kate smiles. "I have made one decision tonight." Kate rubs her hands together. "The hell with stock options. I'm gonna fight the system." Norma jumps up and grabs Kate's hand. "Let's do some system fighting."

Kate is incredulous, "Right now? It's after ten!"

"No time like the present," Norma responds, then adds, "...since my candle really has burned out." Kate smiles. Norma continues, "Let's call Beth. I'm sure we won't be interrupting anything!"

Kate drives the women in her small black BMW sedan. Norma's in the front and Beth lounges in the back. Beth is gleeful. "Sounds like a plan to me. I feel like Catwoman, out on the town."

Kate says, "Actually, Norma, we've elected you to be Catwoman since you can slip in and out unnoticed..."

In the mall parking lot, a few cars are parked in the far reaches of the huge lot. Kate pulls halfway between the entrance to Keith's Cafeteria and the dumpster shed. Kate says,

"Norma, Beth and I were livid to find out that the cafeteria throws away leftovers because of some lame Health Department ruling." Beth adds, "What a waste! The shelter could've put that food to good use." Kate interjects, "The one guy who agreed with us said that they even put the leftovers in big to-go boxes so they won't stink up the dumpster."

Beth points to a young man wearing a gray jumpsuit and listening to small headphones that are wrapped around his long blondish hair. He pushes an industrial strength trashcan from the back of the Keith's to the nearby dumpster. Beth cheers, "Dinner is served."

Kate opens her car door and pops the hood. She exits the car. "Young man, could you help us?" He moves his headphones slightly and looks around to make sure he's the one being addressed. Figuring there might be a couple of bucks in it, he pushes the large trashcan over to Kate's car. "What's the problem?" Kate answers, bewildered, "The car won't start." Kate walks around to the back and opens the trunk. "All I have is a jack. Will that help?" Kate all but flutters her eyelashes in this "helpless female" routine. The young man gets in behind the wheel, next to Beth. Kate hands him the keys as Norma "pops" out of the car and begins loading the boxes of food onto a plastic tarp in the trunk.

The key won't fit the ignition. Without speaking, the young man hands the wrong key back to Kate through the window. She hands him another key. The car starts on the first try. "My hero," Beth says flatly. The young man gets out of the car. Kate hands him a twenty dollar bill and then gets in behind the wheel. "Anytime, Ma'am." The young man pockets the twenty. "You sure I can't unzip your purse for you or adjust your outside mirror?" He laughs lightly and pushes the much lighter trash can toward the dumpster.

Norma slams the trunk. The young man looks around, startled. Norma "pops" back into the car. He mutters under his breath, "Fuckin' loonies...but hey, a twenty dollar bill for nothin'."

Kate turns to look behind her before backing the BMW up to a loading dock. Beth gets out of the car and walks up the few stairs. She shifts her weight from foot to foot after ringing the buzzer by the back door. Conner Street Shelter is printed across the door in peeling paint. A stooped, elderly man wearing a hair net and a white canvas apron over his jeans and T-shirt opens the door. Beth points and then leads the way to the car.

Kate pops the trunk latch. She then gets out of the car and helps carry the containers of food up to the door. The man says, "Had a big party, you said?" Beth smiles. "We just didn't want to see all this food go to waste." The man flashes a gap-toothed smile. "Believe me, nothing goes to waste around here."

Kate slows the BMW to a stop in front of a store with "LaLa Land! L.A.'s Premiere Consignment Shop" scrawled across the front window. Beth says, "I should do all my shopping late at night. Last time we were here we had to park three blocks away."

The ladies enter the shop. They pass Brad, a dazzling sales clerk/actor wannabe, who is wearing one of Robin Williams' Hawaiian shirts. Brad is flirting with Kris, the emaciated Goth girl behind the counter. Beth (accidentally on purpose) spills her bottled water down her leg. Brad turns.

"Need some help?" Beth slowly runs her hand up her leg, lingering high up on her inner thigh. She answers, "I'm fine, thanks. It seems I'm a little...wet."

Brad hands Beth a Kleenex, then returns to his flirtation with Kris.

On their way toward the back of the store, Kate pulls out a leather mini skirt. "I love this." She reads from the tag, "It's from Barbara Bach. You know, she's married to Ringo." Beth shakes her head. "Paul, all the way!" Kate says to Norma, "Ringo and Paul were in The Beatles." Norma says, "Sure, with George and John, such sweet guys. I happened to be in Processing when John arrived, and everyone in line chanted 'Give Peace a Chance!' "

The ladies make their way to the Halloween costumes, in particular, the Marilyn section. Kate pulls out cheap but authentic-looking replicas of Marilyn's iconic white dress from *The Seven Year Itch* and a couple of the pink strapless gowns from *Gentlemen Prefer Blondes*. Norma is astonished. "Women actually dress like me for Halloween?" Beth answers, "Not just the women!"

In mere moments, Beth and Kate step out of their dressing rooms. Kate is in the pink strapless gown. She has added a platinum wig and a sparkly rhinestone necklace. Beth wears the white dress. Norma spins in place and then she's also in the pink gown. Norma immediately goes into Marilyn-mode. Kate mimics her poses. Beth says, "You two could be sisters!" Kate does her best imitation of a Marilyn pout, and they all laugh.

Back in their street clothes, the ladies pass Brad, who is still working on Kris. Norma squeezes between Brad and Kris to hop on the edge of the counter. As Brad leans in, Norma raises her leg between his. Brad leans into Norma's slow, even movements, riding her foot until he buckles. Kris says, "Better get your ass in gear, Brad. Morty's watching." Brad looks up, glassy-eyed. He sucks in air and throws his head back as Morty approaches.

Norma turns toward Beth and Kate. "And to think, he's getting paid for this."

Morty's gigantic bulk casts a shadow in front of Brad. Morty asks, "Taking a little break, Brad?"

Norma, Kate and Beth leave the store. A haze forms at the front window. Norma materializes. She blows Brad a kiss and then walks away.

Brad turns to Morty. "Did you see that? It was Marilyn Monroe!"

Morty answers, "Yeah, and I'm River Phoenix. Back to work, jerk-off."

The ladies are in Kate's car that is parked on a side street. Kate leans over the steering wheel, laughing. Beth wipes tears from her face and Norma leans back on the front seat.

Kate suggests, "Maybe Norma could waltz into a massage parlor and make off with the night's receipts." Norma isn't paying attention. She's distracted by a star, twinkling brightly for attention. Beth says, "Guess she's gone again. Her battery must be running low."

Norma telepathically says to Peg, "I know it's almost the fifth, Peg. Just give me a break." Norma snaps back to the present. "OK, ladies, have we come up with anything? How about re-distributing some drug money?"

Beth answers, "About four blocks over is goddamned

drug central, but I don't think we want to pull the car stalling routine over there."

Kate drives around the area. The dashboard clock reads 12:04 a.m. Beth shouts, "Happy Birthday, Kate." Norma leans forward and pats Kate's arm. She sings in a breathy, wisp of a voice, "Happy Birthday, Madame President, Happy Birthday to you." They all laugh, then Norma gets serious again. "Pull over, Kate. You all can wait across the street at Denney's, and we'll have some birthday pancakes when I get back from drug town."

Norma "pops" out of the car. "I'll be back by twelve thirty. Just direct me and I'll bring back the goods."

Beth laughs. "Is that a line from one of your movies?"

Norma scoffs. "You must be joking. I never remembered my lines back when I needed them, much less forty years later." Norma says, "Don't worry about me. I'm a big spirit. I can take care of myself."

Norma stands in front of an abandoned warehouse. Three young men in their late teens enter as two men in their mid-to-late twenties stagger out. A tough, muscled man with a shaved head stands inside the door, blocking entry. Norma walks right through the muscle-bound man, into the building. As she squeezes by, he looks around. Satisfied that no one has gotten past him, he resumes his slouch.

Inside the building, a deserted, open office space serves as a shooting gallery. Dilapidated half-walls separate the space, with the lobby area housing twenty or so men and women in varying stages of euphoria. Discarded needles litter the floor and smoke fills the air. Windows are covered in war-time heavy draping. The only light in the room is the eerie glow of cheap, waxy candles that line the floors.

Norma walks toward the back, passing another threatening man in camouflage fatigues who serves as lookout. Norma delicately steps over bodies. Lookout man kicks a reed-thin woman who has slumped over in the hallway. He asks, "Whaddya want for twenty bucks, lady? This isn't the Holiday Inn. Take your whoring outside. You spent your twenty already."

Norma enters a long, narrow room that obviously served as the previous tenant's break room. There's a sad little microwave on one counter and a dorm-sized refrigerator against the other wall. All around are remnants of Human Resource-type flyers peeling off the walls—rah-rah sayings like "There is no 'I' in TEAM" and "Make it a TEAM effort" that are totally out of place in this dreary room.

The room is now occupied by two tall fully-armed men standing behind a small, bookish man in his early twenties seated at the long table.

Hanging behind the table on a slime-green wall are the doctored remnants of the former tenant's "gung-ho" posters that have been updated by the current residents. The poster that brags "Sixty-Four Days Without An Accident. Let's Keep It That Way!" now has a hypodermic sticking into the pictured patient's leg cast. "Breaks are Limited to Ten Minutes" has the word "CRANK" written into the worker's cartooned daydream.

The bookish money counter puts stacks of bills in piles. The bills cover the entire surface of the long table. Norma walks behind the table and runs her fingernail up the muscled arm of one of the bodyguards. He doesn't even flinch. She leans over the small money-counting man. He snaps back and yells at one of the guards, "Stay off my goddamned neck. Just stand back and watch the door." The two guards look at one another and turn face-front again. One gives the small man the finger and the other gives him a clenched fist salute, behind his back. Norma exits the room and walks up the back stairs. She "pops" through the locked door on the landing.

Now in the upstairs room, Norma watches as a few young workers fill small vials with crack cocaine. Posted at the door and one boarded-up window are armed guards. The window guard picks up one of the vials. The door guard stares him down, then rubs his fingers against his thumb, indicating money. The window guard throws a twenty dollar bill down on the table.

Norma puckers up and blows. The contents of the table are strewn all over the place in the whirlwind. The workers duck under the table as the guards try to stop the drugs from heading down the floor registers. Norma says, "Twenty dollars for a quick high..." She "pops" through the wall, then continues, "and a slow death."

Kate taps the dashboard. Beth picks at her nails. The dashboard clock reads 12:16 a.m. Beth asks, "Can you even believe that we're sitting here waiting for Marilyn Monroe to rob a drug lord?" Kate laughs. "The entire time since my accident has seemed so strange, so surreal, it's hard for me to say what sounds real anymore." Beth responds. "Coincidentally, it's also the anniversary of Norma's death. Didn't that newspaper headline say August 5th?"

Kate shakes her head. "Like I said, this whole thing is so surreal."

Beth counters, "Speaking of surreal, wanna go over to Denney's and have a Rootin' Tootin' roundup with scrambled eggs and pancakes?"

On the first floor of the abandoned building, Norma kneels beside a slight teenage girl with jet black hair in a short pixie style while a young man in an oversized army jacket tries to revive her. She hangs limp in his arms. Her head shakes like a rag doll as he jostles her.

An older toothless man in the shadows leans forward. "Give it up, man! She's a goner." The young man yells, "Carrie Lynn!" He tries to stand but his legs buckle under him. The man in the shadows continues, "Check her pockets. Maybe she's holding."

Norma watches as Carrie Lynn's glowing sunburst floats away from her body that is slumped on the floor, and heads up through the ceiling. Norma says, "I'd go with you, Carrie Lynn, but Peg may not let me leave again. Your Aunt Carol will meet you on the other side."

Beth looks out the back window. The dashboard clock reads 12:26 a.m. Beth shouts, "Here she comes, empty-handed. Can we go home now?" Norma "pops" into the car. "Ladies, there's enough money in there to house a city full of homeless people, but I left after watching a fifteen-year-old girl die. There has to be another way to get to their money!" Kate shivers and then starts the car. Kate says, "Okay if we skip the pancakes? I don't feel much like celebrating." They travel in silence down deserted streets. Norma asks, "Could I ask a favor?"

Kate pulls up to a parking lot and stops the car. The dashboard clock reads 12:38 a.m. Norma "pops" out of the car while Kate and Beth again wait. Norma says, "I'll only be a moment."

Norma "pops" through the outer brick wall of the building. Inside, she bumps directly into Humphrey Bogart. "My God! Sorry, Bogie."

Norma is smack-dab in the middle of the Wax Museum's display of Bogart and Hepburn from *The African Queen*. Norma moves quickly past the next exhibit—Michael Jackson in tiptoe pose from the "Billie Jean" video, then the next— Marlon Brando in his torn T-shirt from *A Streetcar Named Desire*. She heads down the hallway, passing Warren Beatty in his yellow *Dick Tracy* trench coat and Liz Taylor in full glory as *Cleopatra*. Norma touches Cleo's gold-banded headdress. The next is Bette Davis from *All About Eve*. Norma says, "Fasten your seatbelts. It's gonna be a bumpy night."

The next display is Marilyn Monroe over the subway grate in *The Seven Year Itch*. "How're you doing, Marilyn?" Norma inquires. She stands close and inspects the wax features. "Nice, very nice." Norma runs her hands through the wax figure's hair and then slowly down the body. "Isn't that what they always said?"

Norma circles the wax figure, darting in and out of the pose. She "pops" into the figure, moving and shifting its arms. Norma momentarily maintains the original pose, holding her skirt down from the subway breeze, then "pops" out again. "Peg was right. Marilyn's no longer comfortable for me."

Kate and Beth are half asleep in the front seat of the car. There's a slight tapping on the passenger side window. Beth jumps a foot, then acknowledges Norma. Norma "pops" into the car's backseat and Kate pulls out of the lot.

At the stoplight, Kate turns on the overhead light. She breaks down laughing and points to Beth. Beth jumps, "What is it? A spider? Shit! I hate spiders." Kate laughs, "You have on two different shoes." Beth leans back and puts her feet up on the dash. "No way!" She sees clearly that she does have on two different shoes. "Well, I'll be damned! A navy Liz and a black Esprit. But they're in entirely different places in my closet." Norma adds, "Maybe Drew's been reorganizing." Beth smiles. "He must be getting playful." Norma suppresses a laugh.

Kate asks, "Rebellion in the ranks? Must be tough to strive for perfection." Beth answers, "If it means getting laid by my husband, I'll never match again." Kate says, "Guess the shelter residents will be well-dressed this winter, since you'll be donating all your coordinated outfits."

Norma leans against the front seat. "One last favor?"

Beth says sternly, "Pushy old broad, isn't she?"

Norma responds, "Just a quick side trip to the hospital. Someone needs a little comforting. It won't take long."

Inside the doctor's lounge, Todd is alone in the room. He's on the phone. Norma "pops" through the wall and stands in the dim light. Todd says, "We had him, but the umbilical cord..." Todd listens for a moment to the person on the phone, then continues, "Yeah, in about forty minutes." There's a slight pause, and then Todd says, "Love you, too."

Norma stands next to Todd as he hangs up the phone and gets into his bunk. She sits on the edge of his bed. Todd tosses and turns. He throws an arm across Norma's legs and sobs against her. Norma pats Todd and wipes a tear from her face.

Kate pulls into Beth's driveway. The exterior of the house is surprisingly homey, with a wraparound porch and wildflowers lining the front walkway. The porch-light glow illuminates the front porch, and Kate's car sitting in the drive.

Beth is outside the car, leaning into Norma's open window. Norma encourages Beth, "Just try initiating it again, but this time without the criticism." Beth crosses her fingers and walks away from the car. "Wish me luck, ladies."

Kate and Norma sit on Kate's deck. They're side by side, holding hands and rocking, oblivious to the darkening storm clouds. Kate says, "We sure made a connection, didn't we? It's like we've known each other for a lifetime."

Norma answers, "You're very strong, Kate. You may soon—very soon—be tested, but you'll find the strength." Kate puts her finger over Norma's mouth to quiet her. "I don't need to know what's ahead. Whatever it is, we'll face it."

Norma adds, "And conquer it."

"I wish you could stay and help," Kate says as she starts crying. Norma comforts her. Kate apologizes, "Raging hormones. I can't get a grip. You know that I want you to go on to whatever rewards are waiting." Kate rubs her eyes and sniffs loudly. "Can you ever come back?" "No," Norma answers. Kate slumps in her chair. Norma continues, "But that's good. I mean, I won't ever come back as Norma but we'll meet again. We were destined to make a difference in each other's lives."

Kate straightens. "It's like my Mommy's abandoning me. The pull is that strong." Norma cries softly. "I might have been called Mommy if I hadn't died that night, thirty-seven years ago tonight." Tears run down Kate's face. "That's when I was born, thirty-seven years ago tonight."

"I know," Norma says softly. "I was there." Kate looks confused. "You were there when I was born? But how?" Norma continues. "I wasn't exactly there. Look, I know that you've been through quite a shock, but there's something I need to tell you." Kate braces herself.

Norma begins, "In this wondrous universe what's important is making a connection with another person." Kate pats Norma's hand. "When I died, I was greeted just like you were greeted by your grandmother. There was a spirit in Admissions who told me that I also brought with me...to the spirit world...the spirit of my unborn child. I wasn't aware that I was carrying a baby from the love of my life. Since I could no longer be that child's mother, the spirit in Admissions gave me the names of two families who were about to give birth, one in Louisville, Kentucky and one in Ohio, and told me I could choose which family to send the spirit of my child to be born into. I chose the family in Louisville."

Kate squirms slightly in her chair. "I'm not quite sure where this is going," she says. Norma asks gently, "Can I continue?" Kate nods. Norma says, "I gave my child all the love and blessings I had to give, and then he was born into the Malone family in Louisville, Kentucky...as Kathryn Loyal Malone."

Kate says slowly, "You mean—"

Norma says softly, "I know this is very hard to accept, but you're the closest I've ever come to being a mother. I know that you're not my child, but I've grown so much in my time with you, and I hope you feel the same way."

Kate smiles slightly. "I'm on brain overload now, since the accident and the pregnancy, so it may take me a while to process all this, but I want you to know that I would have been proud to have had you as my mother."

Norma wipes a tear from her cheek. "Kate, I have work ahead of me. I'm open now to the path ahead; you've found yours. You were born ready; I needed a little push. You've shown me that while there's nothing wrong with being beautiful on the outside, your family is the true reflection of the beauty you have within you." Kate runs her hands across her abdomen. "Is it ever. And you've taught me the value of life." Contented, Kate leans back and closes her eyes.

Norma says, "I can move on now. I've experienced motherhood in all its glory, and it is..."

Kate interrupts and says sleepily, "Glorious!"

Norma leans in and hugs Kate. Kate clutches her tightly. She says, "I'm gonna rest here for about ten more minutes, then head upstairs. You sure you're okay?"

Norma stands. "I'm just fine. It's you I was concerned about." Kate says, "Who wouldn't be thrilled to have been given such a tremendous gift. I was given the spirit of a very loved, very much wanted child in order to start my life in love."

Norma looks toward the black sky of storm clouds that is slowly lightening to gray. One lone star twinkles. Norma says telepathically, "I'm ready now, Peg. I know. I'll never be her Mother, but I am a good, close friend." The star blinks madly. Norma continues, "Maybe she'll draw strength from our time together." The star dims. "I know. She'll need it."

Chapter Nine

Doggie Daze

Just before dawn, Norma stands next to a candy-apple-red Pooch Palace van that is parked in the shadows of a dingy side street. The van's back doors are wide open. Two muscled guards load dog carriers into the van. A yelping dog is in each carrier. When the men finish loading, Muscleman One throws the car keys to Muscleman Two. Norma reaches up and grabs the keys in midair. She jumps in the driver's seat before the men can figure out what has happened to the key. The men are looking on the ground as the van starts up. Norma peels off. The two men look at one another and panic.

Kate is sleeping soundly in the rocker on her back deck. Ray taps gently on her arm to awaken her. He looks up at the graying sky. "Better get inside or you'll get drenched." Kate stretches, then slowly stands. She hugs Ray. "Have I told you lately how much you mean to me?" Ray pulls away from the hug so he can look into Kate's face. Before he can answer, she continues, "And how glad I am that we found one another?" Ray starts to speak but she continues, "And how I want this baby." Ray hugs her close. She asks, "Wonder how the kids will feel?" Ray hesitates to make sure she's finished, then finally he's able to answer. "Oh, resentful, jealous, proud, then thrilled." Kate and Ray kiss.

The Pooch Palace van pulls into a residential side street and stops at the curb. Norma "pops" out of the van and goes around to the back to open the door.

She turns and manifests herself into Kate in the Nike "Just Do It" T-shirt and biker shorts. She reaches in and opens a dog carrier. A small cairn terrier jumps out and races around inside the van. Norma reaches into the carrier. Taped to both sides are hefty envelopes stuffed with cash. Norma opens another carrier. A small cocker spaniel rushes out and sniffs the terrier. Norma frees several more small dogs, and retrieves several more stuffed envelopes. Soon there are twelve dogs running in the van and twenty-four cash-filled envelopes in Norma's hands. Norma gently says "Stay," and each dog stops in its tracks. She then says "Down," and each dog lies down.

Norma returns to the driver's seat. Several of the dogs bark. Norma only has to say "No," and the barking immediately stops. Norma consults the yellow pages directory that sits on the seat next to her, its phone booth chain still dangling. She says to herself, "Conner, where's Conner Street?" Norma drives down side streets, slowing to look at street signs.

Outside the abandoned warehouse/crack house, the man guarding the front door holds a car door open on the Town Car for the money-counting man. Mr. Money Counter exits the building in a rush and pushes past the guard to enter the car. He leans forward to speak to the driver. "You'd better find that van, and you'd better find it fast." The guard closes the car door. The Town Car speeds off. The warehouse guard turns to the two muscled men, skulking in the doorway. The guard says to the two musclemen, "You boys better hope he finds that van, and the cash!"

Inside the Town Car, Mr. Money Counter taps his bejeweled fingers against the glass separating him from the driver. The driver lowers the glass. Money Counter says, "Cover this whole city if you have to." The driver answers, "This is strictly amateur stuff, Boss. We'll find it."

Norma pulls the van into a Taco Bell parking lot. A gray-haired man loads newspapers into a machine near the street, then gets in his white compact car and drives away. Moments later, a lean dark-haired man runs in place as he buys a newspaper from the machine. He sees the Pooch Palace van drive by, but there's no driver. He shakes his head, grabs his paper and continues his early morning run.

Inside Beth's bathroom, Drew and Beth, in robes and still wet from their shower, slump against the bathroom wall, laughing. They're surrounded by unfolded white towels.

In the linen closet the once regimented toiletries are now in disarray. Drew hugs Beth and inquires, "This mess doesn't bother you even a little bit?" Beth hugs him back. "Not in the slightest." As Beth states her denial, she reaches across behind Drew and straightens a framed print on the wall that's hanging off balance. Drew watches her in the vanity mirror and smiles. "I believe you." Drew playfully lifts a strand of wet hair and kisses Beth's neck.

In the Taco Bell parking lot, the Pooch Palace van is backed into the shadows, only its grill sticking out. Inside the van, Norma reaches for a leash. She exits the van. Her step is self-assured, sure-footed, her gaze determined. She walks a sheltie on a leash toward a phone booth down the block. The gray-haired newspaper man pulls his white car over to her at the curb. "Better be careful out on the streets this time of morning. Pretty deserted." Norma smiles back at him. He drives off.

Moments later, a yellow cab pulls up outside the Conner Street Shelter. Norma gets out of the cab, leans into the open window and pays Desmond, the cabbie, a young black man with long dreadlocks. "Desmond, could you watch Pokie for me? I should be just a few minutes," she asks sweetly. Desmond looks around at the well-behaved sheltie who sits at attention on the back seat. "Sure," he answers. Norma as Kate walks up the stairs to the entrance. She takes a thick envelope out of her waistband and enters the shelter.

After a ten minute wait, Desmond is getting antsy. He opens his cab door and whistles for the dog to get out of the cab. The dog won't budge. Desmond gets out of the cab and opens the back door. "Come on, Pokie," he pleads. The dog's not going anywhere. Desmond reaches in to try and grab Pokie. Stuck in the dog's collar is a thick envelope. Desmond removes it from the collar. Across the front of the envelope is written, "Thanks, Desmond." He reaches in and pulls out a stack of twenty dollar bills. A big smile breaks across his face. "Well, Pokie," he says, "I guess you're goin' home with me." He gives Pokie a big hug and scratches him behind the ears, then shuts the back door, walks around to the front, and gets in the cab. As soon as he is seated and has the key in the ignition, he looks back over his shoulder at Pokie. Pokie barks, as if to say, "Okay, let's go." Desmond laughs, and drives away.

Money Counter Man pushes a button on his armrest so the Town Car driver can hear him speak. "A fucking candy-apple-red van with Pooch Palace splashed across the side just disappears into the dawn?" The driver answers, "Sir?" Money Counter lashes out. "Never mind. Just keep your fucking mind on the road. And find that fucking van."

Norma sits in the back of a Checker cab with a small Pekinese curled up in her lap. The female driver has light braided hair, very different from the picture on the passenger side visor that shows Jenine Peterson with dark curly shoulder-length hair. The cab pulls up to a hospice center. Norma pays Jenine and then opens her door. Norma asks sweetly, "Jenine, would you mind watching Sparky? I'll only be a moment and he's a real sweetie." Jenine grunts. Norma takes this as a yes. She adjusts the thick envelope sticking from her belt and enters the hospice door. Jenine adds, "The meter's running."

In a grimy and noisy cab dispatch center, a burly overweight man in a navy blue work shirt with Vinnie sewn on the pocket flap speaks into a headset. "Just got a call from Jenine. Little dog this time, smushed-in kinda face." He listens for a moment. "Yeah, Pekinese. That's it. I don't know what's going on. Brad over at Yellow Cab said they've had about three so far this morning." Vinnie takes a quick bite from a donut. "Yeah, wish I was driving a cab this morning. Sounds like it's paying pretty good out there."

Marty, the red-faced fortyish US Cab driver, scans the streets and talks to his dispatcher. The cabbie says, "Man, wish

I could spot her. Sign me up for a quick thousand just to do a little dog-sitting!"

At a 4-way stop at the corner, a lady driving a Yellow Cab sits at the intersection; a young woman driving a Checker cab sits to her right; Marty in his US Cab sits to her right, and a guy driving an American Cab sits to his right. They're all cruising the area, on the lookout for the generous dog lady in the Nike shirt. Word travels fast.

Several blocks away in the Taco Bell lot, Norma exits the van with seven dogs on leashes. She untangles them, leaves the lot and walks toward the intersection. She stops to lean down and pet the Yorkie. "Got yourself all tangled up here, baby." While down on one knee, Norma puts down a stack of bills under her foot. She stands and waits for the light to change. As she steps away, the bills begin scattering in the morning breeze. It's early yet but there's still traffic. Cars screech to a stop behind Norma. She continues walking, then turns to glance back. She sees drivers leaving their cars in the middle of the street to jump out and grab their share of the cash blowing in the wind.

Norma nonchalantly turns right, goes to the next block and turns right again. She bends down to kiss the whimpering little black lab puppy. He's now tangled up in his leash. "Let me get that for you, little buddy." Norma tosses a stack of bills into a storefront alcove. As she walks away, she again hears cars stopping. She turns to see the activity. The long black Town Car weaves around all the cars stopped in the middle of the road. The Town Car heads straight toward Norma. She ducks into the next side street. It's a dead end.

Blaire and Brady stare at their separate cereal boxes

while Kate unloads the dishwasher. There's a small kitchen TV that's on but the volume is low. On the screen, the bubbly young anchorwoman with highlighted hair talks directly into the camera. "The dog-loving benefactor has been distributing large sums of money to local charitable organizations. Each cabbie got a pedigreed dog, and a little over one thousand dollars!" Melissa pauses for effect, and then continues, "Now our own Chad Ballou reports live from the Conner Street Shelter. Take it away, Chad."

The screen changes to the exterior of the shelter, grayed by the overcast skies. Chad Ballou, Channel Five's tan, blonde, thirty-year-old reporter, who wears a beautifully-cut gray designer suit and starched blue shirt, and looks like he belongs in a toothpaste commercial, takes a valuable moment of air time to flash the audience his breathtaking smile. He stares intently into the camera, his brown eyes smoldering, then he begins, "Eyewitness Five's Chad Ballou here." Chad throws his shoulders back and stands taller, then looks around toward the building behind him, "Reporting live from the Conner Street Shelter, scene of one of this morning's mysterious charitable contributions." Chad pushes the microphone into the face of an obviously uncomfortable, bookish man in an ill-fitting suit standing next to him. "I'm here with Peter Williams, director of the shelter. Mr. Williams, can you tell our viewers something about your benefactor?" Mr. Williams is obviously nervous to be on camera. He clears his throat and begins, "At about five-thirty this morning, a lady walked in and gave one of our breakfast volunteers an envelope of cash. That's about it. I'm sorry. I'm very nervous." Chad reassures him. "Mr. Williams, try to calm down. You're doing fine. So was there nothing about where the money came from or who this woman was?"

Mr. Williams nervously shakes his head. Chad asks, "How much money was in the envelope?" Mr. Williams replies immediately, "Twenty-seven thousand dollars, Mr. Ballou." Chad gives a big thumb's up to the camera. "This is Eyewitness Five's Chad Ballou reporting from the Connor Street Shelter, scene of a twenty-seven thousand dollar money drop earlier this morning by the city's silent benefactor, a dark-haired woman in a Nike T-shirt and biker shorts. Be on the lookout, ladies and gentlemen."

Kate is rinsing cereal bowls at the sink. She says to the kids, "It's almost eight o'clock. We'd better get moving." The phone rings. Kate picks up the cordless phone and turns off the TV. "Hello. I know, Beth. I saw it on the earlier broadcast. It's bound to be Norma. I haven't seen her all morning." Kate laughs. "Right. Robin Hood without the tights."

Beth stands in her bedroom in a black half-slip and black lacy camisole. She lifts her shoulder to hold the phone as she slips on her black-and-white herringbone skirt. "I'm glad she went alone. I had quite enough adventure for one night, and that includes after I got home. I'll tell you later. Gotta run. Some of us have to go back to work, you know." Beth hangs up the phone and goes into her walk-in closet.

Kate grabs her keys and purse and ushers the kids out the kitchen door to the garage.

Beth buttons her white silk shirt as she watches the bedroom TV. She grabs the remote and changes the channel. Mr. Williams from the shelter is speaking with another reporter, an attractive Hispanic lady in a black suit with a red silk shirt under the shawl collar of the jacket. Beth says to the screen, "Nice jacket, Rosita." On the TV, Mr. Williams has obviously become more comfortable on camera, or he's much more relaxed being next to Rosita than Chad. He says, "She was of average height, with brown hair." Beth sits on the edge of the bed and listens intently. "And she was wearing a T-shirt from one of the sneaker companies." Mr. Williams is gaining confidence. His voice has stabilized. "Oh, another thing. She did say her name was Kate. That's all. Just Kate."

Beth grabs her phone and dials. She says into the phone, "So the Davises aren't available to take my call?" Beth hangs up the phone.

At the dead-end street, Norma takes the leashes off all the dogs and releases them. They sit right at her feet. "Run along now. I can't take you with me." Norma nudges them gently with her foot. They don't move an inch. Car brakes squeal loudly.

The Town Car pulls to a screeching halt in front of Norma and the dogs. Norma shakes her finger vigorously. The driver turns back to Mister Money Counter. "Watch this one, boss. She looks like a crazy." Money Counter replies, "No shit, Sherlock! What was your first clue? She has to be crazy to pull a stunt like this. But she has a little something that belongs to me! Or she did before giving it away."

The driver shakes his head. "That guy on the radio said cabbies were driving all over town looking for her and the dough!"

Money Counter and the driver, a stocky, barrel-chested man in a tight uniform, walk slowly toward Norma. Money Counter calmly asks, "So where's the van?" The driver kicks a dog out of the way. The little Jack Russell terrier whimpers and moans. Norma leans down to comfort the puppy. "You've hurt him." Money Counter grabs at Norma. "He's not the only one who's gonna end up getting hurt." Norma pulls the little dog close to her.

A Yellow cab and Checker cab almost hit one another as they turn into the dead-end side street. The drivers have spotted the "dog lady" with all the ready cash. They pull up and stop suddenly.

Both middle-aged, portly cabbies race out of their cabs toward Norma. They're stopped by Money Counter's driver. Yellow Cabbie asks, "Are we too late?" Checker Cabbie doesn't wait for an answer before asking, "Any money left?"

Money Counter glares at the two cabbies.

Yellow Cabbie says, "There's plenty for all of us." Checker Cabbie adds, "She's been handing out money all morning."

Money Counter grabs for Norma. His driver blocks the cabbies from leaving. Norma spins out of his grasp and fades away. The four men look at one another, disbelieving what they think they've seen.

Two blocks away, a bag lady checks a phone booth's change slot. She's startled as the phone receiver 'jumps" off the hook. The dial moves on its own, first nine, then one, then one. The bag lady runs from the phone booth. A male voice is heard on the hanging receiver. "Nine one one. What's your emergency?" A disembodied female voice answers, "The dog lady with all the money is being chased by a drug lord in a big Lincoln over on Tremont! Hurry!"

The 911 Operator says, "Dogs? Drugs? Hold on, lady. I'll give you the Robbery detail."

All four men search the area for the vanished lady.

Money Counter and his driver look for Norma while the cabbies search for stray hundred dollar bills. The dogs run under the Town Car. The cabbies get down on all fours and whistle for the dogs to come out. Yellow Cabbie whispers to Checker Cabbie, "Dispatch said the dogs had the money on 'em. Let's get our share."

A police car pulls into the dead-end street and stops, blocking the entrance. There's no place for Money Counter and his driver to run. The cabbies are halfway under the Town Car, trying to get the dogs out. Two police officers, a female and a male, slowly get out of their car and approach the cabbies, Money Counter and his driver.

HELLO, NORMA JEAN

Chapter Ten

Tourist Trap

Outside Mann's Chinese Theatre, tourists tentatively place their hands in the handprints of Hollywood's great stars, hoping for a match. The handprints of Marilyn Monroe are darkened; they are the most popular of all.

Norma floats over the congested courtyard. She spins, releasing money into the crowd. People look up toward the sky, grabbing bills. Surprisingly orderly and polite, with no pushing or grabbing, they reach for this wonderful manna from heaven. Norma blows on the bills and they climb higher in the wind to spread further across the city.

At the dead-end street, the bills blow overhead. Money Counter looks up at his money floating by.

Several blocks away, Kate sits at a stoplight as people race across the street. Blaire and Brady strain in their car seats to watch people boost one another up onto signs and into trees to gather the bills that have settled there. The people clutch the found money to their chests.

Kate drives slowly, deliberately. She pulls up alongside the entrance to the dead-end street, which has been closed to traffic by a police car blocking the entry. Kate says to the kids,

"Must be an accident." Kate sees a policeman standing behind two men who are spread-eagled face down against the hood of a big Lincoln Town Car. Several small dogs pace uncertainly at the officer's feet. A policewoman nearby takes notes from two cabdrivers who are both talking excitedly at the same time as they wave their arms wildly about. A woman gets out from under the far side of the Town Car. She's holding an armful of small dogs. The woman stands. It is Norma, as Kate, staring back at Kate.

Beth checks herself in her dresser mirror. Her silk shirt looks wrinkled. Beth only shrugs and tucks in her shirt. "You got laid, didn't you? Who cares about a few wrinkles?" She breaks into a big grin, then turns away from the mirror.

Kate sits dumbfounded at the wheel of her car as she stares ahead at the reflection of herself. She sighs aloud, "Norma, Norma." The kids echo her mockingly, saying "Norma Norma" in sing-songy voices that get louder and louder.

An Eyewitness Five van pulls up to the blocked entry. A cameraman races from the van, Chad Ballou right behind him. They stand close by Norma/Kate. The cameraman checks Chad in the lens, and the interview begins.

Kate takes a deep breath and turns back to the kids. "Wonder if Aunt Beth has any ice cream?" The kids squeal with delight as Kate drives off. Blaire and Brady sing in unison, "Ice cream! Ice cream!"

The Marilyn Monroe *Seven Year Itch* display at the Wax Museum is knocked over by a strong wind. A spinning eddy ripples the folds of the wax figure's white dress.

Kate sits in the window seat of the bay window in Beth's sunny kitchen. Kate's on the phone as Beth enters. "Hey, Birthday Girl, hold that pose. You're glowing." Kate halfheartedly smiles and says into the phone, "Sure, honey. I just seized the opportunity. I'll tell you all about it later." There's a pause and Kate leans back and rolls her eyes. "I love you too, Ray. See you tonight." Kate hangs up the phone. "Guess I'm going to have a lot of explaining to do. I need to call my Mother, I need to..." Beth interrupts, "So, when's the dog lady going to the great fire hydrant in the sky?" Kate laughs. Beth turns on the small TV/VCR that's on her kitchen counter. She inserts the tape and then leans against the kitchen counter for a close look at the screen. Kate objects. "Please! Not again." Beth insists. "Just once more before I leave for the office. What's a few more minutes? It's 9:00. I'm already an hour late."

On the TV screen, Norma/Kate says to Chad, "I just did what any good citizen would've done. We have to start caring about what's going on in our streets today." Chad then looks directly into the camera, all sincerity and warmth. "And there you have it. Kate Davis found a bag of money left behind by a drug dealer. She turned that money into an unexpected blessing for many area charities." He turns to look at Kate and then back to the camera for a close-up. "Kate Davis made a difference today." Chad pauses dramatically for his big finish. "And so can you."

Norma's voice says, "And you will make a difference, Kate." Beth and Kate look around the kitchen for Norma. She's nowhere in sight. Beth turns toward the entryway to her dining room, then jumps back in shock.

Norma is standing in the archway in a filmy white gown. She crosses to the counter and brings a pot of coffee to the table. "I only have a second. It's August fifth. My moment is passing." Norma leans down to kiss Kate on the cheek. "Happy Birthday!"

Beth starts to tuck in her shirt, but decides to leave it the way it is. Kate smiles. Beth grabs her keys. "I'll leave you ladies alone. I'd better get to the office." Beth walks to Norma and kisses her. "Nice work, Norma. It was great meeting you." As Beth leaves the kitchen, she calls into the dining room, "Enjoy your ice cream, kids."

Norma sits down next to Kate. "I just wanted to give you a leg up on righting some of the wrongs out there." Kate smiles. "Thanks." Norma says, "I only gave you direction, just like Ray did years ago. Now it's up to you to find your path." Kate squeezes Norma's hand and asks softly, "Is this really good-bye?" Norma nods. "Peg will send out the hounds."

Outside the bay window sits a little Springer spaniel at attention. Kate says, "Whoever Peg is, looks like she's already sent 'em out." Norma smiles. "I hope he'll find a good home— a home with a big yard, a couple of kids, maybe a baby on the way. Know of anyone?" Kate leans and taps on the window to get the dog's attention. The dog's ears spring up. Kate shouts, "Kids! Come look at the puppy."

Norma taps the window. The little spaniel dances with delight. The kids race into the room, see the dog through the window, and immediately run out the door. They plop down on the patio, sitting cross-legged. The frisky puppy jumps from lap to lap. Kate goes to the door. "Looks like the puppy has found a new family. Let's call him Norman, kids, after a very dear friend of Mommy's."

Norma stands and walks behind Kate. She puts her hands on Kate's shoulders. "I wish we could've had more time together." Norma's face begins aging, ever so slightly. Her hair begins to turn from platinum blonde to platinum gray, but loses none of its luster. Norma rubs Kate's shoulders. Kate melts under her touch, moving her head to get the maximum effect of the rubdown. Kate moans, "Oh, that's heavenly."

Norma's soft face wrinkles. Her neck is now lined and full.

Kate's head drops. She rolls it side-to-side. "Don't ever stop. That feels so good."

Norma's shoulders lower and slump slightly. Her filmy gown fills out as her hips widen. Norma asks Kate, "Better?"

Kate answers, "Much better. Thanks."

Kate pats Norma's hand, then pulls back slightly as she feels the wrinkled skin. Kate turns slowly to face Norma. She sees Norma now as a still beautiful but slightly plump, elderly, graying woman. Norma's eyes still twinkle with delight. Her wrinkled face is all smiles, framed by a halo of light.

Kate whispers, "Norma Jean, it's really you."

Norma moves quickly to the wall mirror in the hallway. Pleased with the vision, she delicately runs her hand across her brow and admires herself momentarily. She says to her image, "My God! I look like my sister Berniece would have looked at this age. Now this is a truly beautiful woman." Before turning to Kate, Norma moves her hands down her ample hips. "Pretty nice, and I never believed I could age gracefully. Not bad for seventy-something!"

Kate's voice cracks as she says, "Not bad at all. Now your beauty outside matches your beauty inside." Kate joins

Norma. She stands beside her, looking in the mirror.

Norma says, "I once said something like I wanted to have the courage to grow old without a facelift; that it might be easier to die young than to face old age, but then you'd never really know yourself. I think I finally know myself."

The kids run in through the kitchen door. Brady tries to hold the squirming puppy. Blaire says, "Raining, Mommy." Kate takes Norman from them. The puppy playfully licks Kate's neck. "Take him in Aunt Beth's garage, kids. We don't want him having a little accident in here on Beth's nice floor." Blaire pleads, "Can we keep him?" Brady chimes in, "Can we?" Kate answers, "I'll call and check with Daddy in a little while, but I think it'll be all right." The kids squeal. Kate puts the puppy down on the floor. Brady asks, "Can he sleep in my room?" Blaire corrects him. "My room!" "We'll see," Kate says.

Norma Jean manifests herself and joins Kate at the table. Kate continues, "Kids, for now, get him in the garage." The kids race out of the kitchen. They chase Norman as they pass Norma. Kate says, "Kids, thank Nanny for the puppy." The kids hug Norma around the waist. Norma breathes in the memory. "Thanks, Nanny," Brady says. Blaire adds, "Thank you, Nanny!" Norma wipes the tears from her eyes. Her voice cracks as she says, "Nanny...Nanny thanks you for giving Norman such a loving home." Kate says to Norma, "Norma, I wanted you to hear what it might sound like to be called Nanny." Norma beams. Kate says softly, "It looks like you're ready to go on."

Beth's phone rings. The answering machine kicks on, "You have reached Beth & Drew. You know the drill. Wait for the tone." Then there's a loud beep. Beth's voice says, "Kate, pick up. If you're still there, pick up the phone."

Kate reaches for the phone. She says to Norma. "Beth always has such perfect timing."

Beth sits in a large conference room. She's watching a big wall television. Beth says, "Kate, before she leaves, you might want to ask Norma what you're supposed to do about drug dealers that may just want their money back. They just said on CNN that..."

In Beth's kitchen, Kate makes a "talky-talky" motion with her hand to Norma. Norma smiles. Kate says, "Thanks for calling, Beth. I'll tell her."

Beth says, "Kate, you're in danger! Don't you see that? Money Counter may be in jail but he has plenty of guys still out on the street who want his money back!"

Kate answers, "She has to go now, Beth. Thanks for letting me know, but it sounds like they'll be behind bars for a long, long time." Kate hangs up the phone. She stands and opens the garage door. The kids rush after Norman into the garage.

Norma hums *Moonlight Sonata*. Kate hugs her close. Kate says, "You're right. Not a drop of Marilyn left."

Norma says, "Guess I don't need stage direction any more. Looks like I might have figured this out for myself...finally."

Kate nods. "You've worked hard for this moment. Is it everything you hoped it would be?"

Norma's aging face brightens. "It's pure heaven."

Kate kisses Norma. Norma moves away. "As your Mr. John so beautifully sang, my candle burned out long ago. It's time for me to go." Norma clutches her heart and offers it to Kate. "You know I leave my heart with you." Kate shudders.

"Good-bye, my friend." Norma moves closer to the door. "You're the closest I ever came to having a daughter."

Norma "pops" through the bay window.

Kate goes out the door and stands on Beth's patio in the pouring rain. A strong gust of wind blows Norma into a tailspin. She spins upward in the whirlwind, transforming into her former gauzy spirit figure, afloat in the threatening sky.

Kate watches in awe as a golden sunburst lights up the sky. Kate holds her wet hair off her face with one hand. The other is lifted in a triumphant salute, fingers tightly crossed and raised to the pouring skies. Kate wipes the rain and tears from her face. She's sobbing. "Hope your next path is a little less bumpy." She clears her throat and gathers herself in order to continue. "I wish you love for your journey, my friend, my mother in spirit. I hope something wonderful is waiting for you."

Norma shouts toward the sky, "Get her inside, Peg. I don't want my new best friend catching pneumonia."

Kate pulls the car into her garage. She removes Norman from Brady's tight grip and gets the kids out of their car seats. Blaire and Brady excitedly jump out of the car and begin chasing Norman around in the garage. Kate says, "Take Norman out in the back yard, kids. I'm going to unload the car and then get the mail. We'll get Norman settled in his new doggie bed...maybe over in that corner." She points to the far corner of the garage.

Kate removes items from the car: a gigantic bag of puppy chow, a dog bed, a small wire crate and assorted dog toys.

Kate comes in the house through the front door. She's carrying the newspaper and a small stack of mail. She walks through to the kitchen and drops the paper and mail on the counter without looking at them. She goes into the family room, sits down on the couch, and smiles as she watches the kids rolling around on the back lawn.

In the kitchen, on the counter, written across the top of the newspaper, is a scrawled handwritten note:

Hey, Do-Gooder, You Bitch.
We want our money back
—or else!

In the family room, Kate hums the melody from "Candle in the Wind."

HELLO, NORMA JEAN

Epilogue

The Messenger

On a fluffy cloud in the kingdom, an elderly Norma, in a flowing, diaphanous white gown and the mink pillbox hat from *Something's Got to Give,* stands on a raspberry sherbet cloud by a white baby grand piano. The young female student with the jet black pixie hairstyle pounds the keys. The tune is unrecognizable. Norma winces slightly. She says, "Try it again, Carrie Lynn."

The student again plays badly. Norma joins Carrie Lynn on the piano bench. Carrie Lynn turns to her. "He'll never get the message, Norma. I play so badly."

Norma pats her arm. "He's listening, Carrie Lynn. But it must come from inside, from your heart."

Carrie Lynn sniffs. "I want my Dad to know how sorry I am that I let him down. I'm so ashamed that I got messed up with crack and overdosed before he could reach me. I'm so ashamed."

Norma stops her. "He'll hear you, Carrie Lynn, if you play from the heart. And as a very wise lady once said to me, as for shame, it's wasted energy. Just let it go!"

Carrie Lynn tries playing again. It's better, but still hesitant.

Peg floats over to Norma. Norma says, "Carrie Lynn, keep practicing. I'll be right back." Norma motions for Peg to move further away from Carrie Lynn. "Any news?" she asks Peg. Peg shakes her hooded head. "Sounds like a 'no,' I'm afraid. You should know something later today." Norma bites her lip. "I've got to get back to her, Peg. I've made a mess of things. I only wanted to help Kate but I've put her in jeopardy. I never even gave it a thought. How selfish of me."

Peg comforts Norma. "Norma, your motives were pure and generous. You were trying to—"

Norma interrupts, "It doesn't matter what I was trying to do. What I did was create a terrible threat to Kate and to her family. I have to fix it. I just have to."

Peg nods. "You know I'll do all that I can, but the decision certainly doesn't rest with me."

Carrie Lynn plays a decent string of notes. Norma moves her hand in a flowing motion. Her student begins again. She is tense and tight. Norma stands and moves over to Carrie Lynn. She gently puts her hand on Carrie Lynn's shoulder. The student immediately relaxes. Norma encourages her. "From the heart."

Carrie Lynn begins again.

Norma tries again to encourage her. "Release the music."

A beautiful, emotional rendition of "Candle in the Wind" fills the air. Norma moves her gray head to the beat of the music. Carrie Lynn cries. There are tears streaming down her face. "I'm sorry, Daddy, and I love you!"

Norma weeps. "You've broken down the walls, Carrie Lynn."

Carrie Lynn plays on.

Soon, dozens of pianos in all shapes and sizes dot the

horizon. Each student has a teacher standing nearby, floating on a fluffy, pastel cloud. "Candle in the Wind" takes over the skies.

In a wider view of the horizon, hundreds of pianos now fill the skies.

"Candle in the Wind" absorbs all sound, as each student sends a message to their loved ones left behind.

HELLO, NORMA JEAN

PART II

A Retrospective on the Life, Loves and Death of Marilyn Monroe

Nearly 50 years after her tragic death, Marilyn Monroe remains one of the most popular public figures of all time. In *Hello, Norma Jean*, I have created a fictional world in which Marilyn experiences what it might have been like to have a child of her own and to grow old gracefully and accept the true Norma Jean she would have become if society, and her own fragile psyche, had allowed. I hope you have enjoyed reading about her journey and witnessing Norma Jean's growth and transformation as she finally finds peace within herself.

In my sequel, *Calling Norma Jean*, I'm trying to help Norma convince the triumvirate of heavenly hosts: Sanctus, Hosanna, and Benedictus, as well as Dominica, who casts the ultimate deciding vote, to please let her go back again to help Kate. Since Norma's well-intentioned guidance has brought danger to Kate and her family, she pleads to be given another chance on earth. My hope is to have Norma and Kate close this final chapter in August of 2012, as we commemorate the fiftieth anniversary of Marilyn's abrupt exit from this world.

While I do not claim to be a Marilyn Monroe scholar, I did conduct a considerable amount of research in the writing of

Hello, Norma Jean. Although there is a wealth of information available about Marilyn, there are many so-called "facts" about her life that are either contradicted by other "facts" or are otherwise of questionable accuracy. For instance, because there is a photo of Marilyn standing in the sand in which it looks like she has six toes on one foot, it was reported again and again over the years that she did, in fact, have six toes. Her given name "Norma Jeane" has been popularized as "Norma Jean." Her sister, Berniece Baker Miracle has also been shown spelled as Bernice. Marilyn's last name is "Mortenson" on her birth certificate, but "Baker" on her baptismal certificate. Her paternity, as well, has long been in question. Was her biological father Martin Edward Mortenson, her mother Gladys' first husband, or Charles Stanley Gifford, Gladys' co-worker? Marilyn is said to have believed Gifford was her father, having been shown his picture by her mother and been told, "This is your father." Marilyn said that since Gifford's thin moustache somewhat resembled Clark Gable's, she would pretend that Gable was her father. Ironically, years later, Clark Gable would be her co-star in *The Misfits*, which was the last film either of them ever made, Gable having died shortly after filming was completed and Marilyn having died during the filming of *Something's Got to Give*. Her notorious insecurities were said to have originated from a series of foster homes, orphanages, instances of alleged sexual abuse, and her mother's mental illness, but many of the alleged incidents of her childhood are speculative and unverifiable.

Since most information about Marilyn is shrouded in mystery and compounded by conspiracy theories, I have used 'reportedly,' 'alleged' and 'supposed' where needed. I have attempted to corroborate facts when I could. Hopefully the information in this retrospective on the Life, Loves and Death of Norma Jean Baker will help you to arrive at your own conclusions, tentative though they may be.

Disclaimer: This information was gathered from many sources. The author and publisher take no responsibility for the validity of the many claims that are impossible to confirm.

The Creation That Was Marilyn Monroe

Born Norma Jean Baker at 9:30 a.m. on June 1, 1926, in Los Angeles, California, much has been written about Marilyn's early childhood. While many facts like poverty and sexual abuse have long been suspected of possible exaggeration and embellishment, undisputed facts remain: no one ever established the definitive identity of her biological father, and, because of her mother's fragile mental health and financial challenges, Marilyn spent time in foster homes and an orphanage and rarely saw her mother. Touching yet telltale moments include Marilyn questioning why she had to go to an orphanage when she wasn't an orphan at all, she had a mother; yet during an early visit, Marilyn reportedly called her mother, Gladys, 'the lady in the red hat.' Marilyn was also not even aware of her older half sister until Marilyn was 12; they met for the first time when she was 18.

Due to the lack of a father figure, Marilyn spent her entire life in search of a learned male influence.

Marilyn commented later in her life that she was never told she was pretty and that she was never brought up expecting to be happy. She always felt that she was treated differently than other children in the households. She was constantly competing for attention and affection—traits that would later manifest themselves in adult Marilyn.

Money and fame didn't bring Marilyn the stability she so coveted. Her deep-rooted sense of abandonment and betrayal colored choices throughout her short life.

Early Career:

• By 1946, Marilyn had appeared on more than 30 magazine covers.

• In mid-1946, she did a screen test at Twentieth Century Fox and signed a contract (as Marilyn Monroe).

• In 1947, after a couple of small parts in films, Twentieth Century Fox did not renew her contract. She signed with Columbia Pictures, but didn't get any movie roles.

• The first magazine article written about Marilyn was published September 8, 1951, in *Collier's* magazine. The profile, "1951's Model Blonde," was published before her first starring role.

• Marilyn appeared on the cover of the very first *Playboy* magazine in 1953.

Note: The famous nude photo of her taken by Tom Kelley in May 1949 originally appeared on a calendar entitled "Miss Golden Dreams." Hugh Hefner bought the rights to use the photo for $500.

Her reported affair with Johnny Hyde, Executive Vice-President of the prestigious William Morris Agency, helped her land a cameo in the Marx Brothers' *Love Happy* and small parts in noted films, *The Asphalt Jungle* and *All About Eve.* After Hyde's death in 1950, Marilyn signed with Famous Artists who negotiated a seven-year contract with Fox. By the end of 1951, Fox gave her starring roles in *Don't Bother to Knock* and *Monkey Business.*

1950's Print Ads:

- LAH Jewelers
- Rayve Cream Shampoo
- Jon-Joy Cosmetics for Nu-U liquid makeup foundation
- Lustre-Cream Shampoo
- Tru-Glo liquid makeup from Westmore Hollywood Cosmetics

Marilyn made her network television debut on the September 13, 1953, airing of *The Jack Benny Show*. She supposedly received a 1954 Cadillac Series 62 convertible as a gift from Jack Benny after appearing on his show.

Television Commercials:

- 1950's: Union Oil of California
- Mid-2004: Marilyn and Gandhi appeared as futuristic virtual professors delivering lectures.
- In late summer 2009, Marilyn was featured in a "priceless" television commercial along with these other celebrities in classic jeans: Marlon Brando, John Wayne, the Ramones, and Carlos Santana.
- In February 2010, TV ads began running in the UK featuring Marilyn and John Lennon in "Anti-Retro" commercials for Citroën, in which Marilyn appears to say during an interview, "You should create your own icons and way of life, because nostalgia isn't glamorous. If I had one thing to say, it would be, 'Live your life now.' "

Stats:

•The studio listed Marilyn's much-admired measurements as 37-23-36 while her dressmaker claimed they were closer to 35-22-35.

•Blue eyes and reddish-brown hair, dyed blonde.

NOTE: Marilyn's hairdresser early in her career, Sylvia Barnhart, was the first to dye Marilyn's hair blonde. Sylvia died in February 2010.

• 5' 5-1/2" tall

• Size 12 dress (closer to a size 6 in today's sizing); size 8 slacks; size 7 shoes; size 36D bra

• Favorite perfume: Chanel No. 5

Marriages:

Marilyn Monroe Quote: "Before marriage, a girl has to make love to a man to hold him. After marriage, she has to hold him to make love to him."

• Marriage Number One: After many years in and out of foster care and orphanages, she became Norma Jean Dougherty when she married James Dougherty at the age of 16 in June of 1942 reportedly in order to avoid being sent to yet another orphanage. They divorced in December of 1946.

Marilyn Monroe Quote: "My husband and I hardly spoke to each other. This wasn't because we were angry. We had nothing to say. I was dying of boredom."

• Marriage Number ?: It is alleged that Marilyn was

married very briefly to writer Robert Slatzer in October of 1952, but no marriage license has been produced to prove it.

• Marriage Number Two: When she eloped with Joe DiMaggio at age 28 in January of 1954, she became Norma Jean DiMaggio. The couple divorced in October of that same year. Joe was said to have been extremely jealous. He was incensed at the catcalls during the filming of the infamous scene from *The Seven Year Itch* when her dress was curled up around her upper thigh by air from the subway grate. DiMaggio returned to California on August 1, 1962, reportedly because they were going to remarry. Joe was the one who claimed Marilyn's body after her death. He arranged for her funeral and paid for her casket and crypt, and allegedly banned the Kennedys and the Rat Pack members (Frank Sinatra, Sammy Davis, Jr., Dean Martin, Joey Bishop and Peter Lawford) from attending her funeral.

Marilyn Monroe Quote: "I was surprised to be so crazy about Joe. I expected a flashy New York sports type, and instead I met this reserved guy who didn't make a pass at me right away! He treated me like something special. Joe is a very decent man, and he makes other people feel decent too."

Marriage Number Three: Having legally changed her name to Marilyn Monroe in February of 1956 (although she had been using the name publicly since 1946), she became Marilyn Monroe Miller when she married Arthur Miller at age 30 in June of 1956. She converted to Judaism for this marriage. During this union, she had an ectopic pregnancy and at least one miscarriage. They divorced in January 1961.

Marilyn Monroe Quote: "Arthur wouldn't have married me if I had been nothing but a dumb blonde."

At the risk of losing her film audience, Marilyn stood by Arthur Miller when he was subpoenaed in June 1956 by the House Un-American Activities Committee (HUAC). When he refused to name the names of those writers believed to be Communist sympathizers, he was convicted of contempt of Congress. The following year, his conviction was overturned through appeal.

Miller's close friend and Marilyn's supposed lover, renowned stage and film director Elia Kazan, had actually named the names of eight supposed Communists to HUAC in 1952. These eight had been associates and friends of Kazan's from the Group Theater. Many of Kazan's former friends and associates refused to speak with him once he testified, including Miller. Kazan and Miller worked together again after not speaking for many years when Kazan directed the Lincoln Center production of Miller's play, *After the Fall.*

Years later, in 1999, many audience members refused to clap as 89-year-old Kazan received his lifetime achievement Academy Award. Kazan made no mention of HUAC in his acceptance speech.

In January of 1964 Miller's play, *After the Fall*, opened on Broadway. Quentin is believed to have been Arthur Miller himself and beautiful yet childlike Maggie, who disintegrates into alcohol and pills, was widely accepted to have been based on Marilyn, although Miller always denied the association.

Excerpt from "After the Fall:"

> QUENTIN: Maggie, I'm not fighting you for those pills anymore. If you start going under tonight, I'm to call the ambulance. And that means a headline. I've been trying to protect you from the consequences—and myself too. And that turns out to be exactly what I shouldn't have been doing.

In October 2004, when Miller was 89, his last play, *Finishing the Picture*, debuted. This play was loosely based on the making of *The Misfits*. The Marilyn Monroe character is pill-popping Kitty. In the play, Kitty is said to have been "stepping on broken glass since she could walk."

The Fassingers, acting teachers in the play, are surely based on the Strasbergs. Arthur Miller stated in his autobiography, *Timebends*, that the Strasbergs had made him feel locked out.

The Miller character says of Kitty, we simply had "too much hope...we weren't able to save each other."

Miller died the following February.

Children:

Marilyn Monroe Quote: "The thing I want more than anything else? I want to have children. I used to feel for every child I had, I would adopt another."

While I speculate in *Hello, Norma Jean: A Flight of Fantasy with Marilyn Monroe* that Marilyn may have been pregnant when she died, she remained childless throughout her life. She suffered from chronic endometriosis that prevented her from ever carrying a child to term. Reportedly she had several abortions and miscarriages over the years.

Her Death:

A 1982 review (details below) of the original inquest into Marilyn's death concluded that the actress committed suicide or accidentally overdosed, and was not murdered. Rumors that she had been murdered were fueled by careless evidence handling, the disappearance of tissue samples and a delay in securing the scene.

Marilyn spent part of the afternoon of her death with her psychiatrist, Dr. Ralph Greenson, who had been hoping to help break Marilyn's Nembutal habit by switching her to chloral hydrate to help her sleep.

Her internist, Dr. Hyman Engelberg, allegedly said that upon examination to pronounce her death, he saw at her bedside sedatives other than the Nembutal he prescribed. Rumored to be present were Seconals, which may have been purchased by Marilyn during a visit to Mexico, and chloral hydrate.

Marilyn's death certificate stated probable suicide as the cause of death. Her autopsy reveals that her stomach contents were devoid of the residue that would have been left from the forty-plus Nembutals that had been reported as the culprit in her death. It is claimed that the drugs could have been administered through an enema.

The Autopsy:

The preliminary autopsy was conducted by pathologist Dr. Thomas Noguchi, who had joined the Los Angeles County medical examiner's office in 1961. He was subsequently the county's chief coroner from 1967-1982. Marilyn Monroe was his first celebrity autopsy. He would later perform autopsies on Robert F. Kennedy, Sharon Tate, Janis Joplin, Natalie Wood, and John Belushi.

Chief Coroner Theodore Curphey concluded that Monroe died from an overdose of drugs, specifically the sedatives chloral hydrate and a massive overdose of more than 45 phenobarbitals, a short-acting barbiturate under the trade name "Nembutal." Curphey ruled the case "probable suicide."

The full text of the autopsy report is as follows.

Autopsy Report on Marilyn Monroe

Findings:

External examination: The unembalmed body is that of a 36-year-old well-developed, well-nourished Caucasian female weighing 117 pounds and measuring 65-1/2 inches in length. The scalp is covered with bleached blond hair. The eyes are blue. The fixed lividity is noted in the face, neck, chest, upper portions of arms and the right side of the abdomen. The faint lividity which disappears upon pressure is noted in the back and posterior aspect of the arms and legs. A slight ecchymotic area is noted in the left hip and left side of lower back. The breast shows no significant lesion. There is a horizontal 3-inch long surgical scar in the right upper quadrant of the abdomen. A suprapubic surgical scar measuring 5 inches in length is noted. The conjunctivae are markedly congested; however, no

ecchymosis or petechiae are noted. The nose shows no
evidence of fracture. The external auditory canals are not
remarkable. No evidence of trauma is noted in the scalp,
forehead, cheeks, lips or chin. The neck shows no evidence of
trauma. Examination of the hands and nails shows no defects.
The lower extremities show no evidence of trauma.

Body cavity: The usual Y-shaped incision is made to
open the thoracic and abdominal cavities. The pleural and
abdominal cavities contain no excess of fluid or blood. The
mediastinum shows no shifting or widening. The diaphragm is
within normal limits. The lower edge of the liver is within the
costal margin. The organs are in normal position and
relationship.

Cardiovascular system: The heart weighs 300 grams.
The pericardial cavity contains no excess of fluid. The
epicardium and pericardium are smooth and glistening. The
left ventricular wall measures 1.1 cm. and the right 0.2 cm.
The papillary muscles are not hypertrophic. The chordae
tendineac are not thickened or shortened. The valves have the
usual number of leaflets which are thin and pliable. The
tricuspid valve measures 10 cm., the pulmonary valve 6.5 cm.,
mitral valve 9.5 cm. and aortic valve 7 cm. in circumference.
There is no septal defect. The foramen ovale is closed. The
coronary arteries arise from their usual location and are
distributed in normal fashion. Multiple sections of the anterior
descending branch of the left coronary artery with a 5 mm.
interial demonstrate a patent lumen throughout. The
circumflex branch and the right coronary artery also
demonstrate a patent lumen. The pulmonary artery contains no
thrombus. The aorta has a bright yellow smooth intima.

Respiratory system: The right lung weighs 465 grams

and the left 420 grams. Both lungs are moderately congested with some edema. The surface is dark and red with mottling. The posterior portion of the lungs show severe congestion. The tracheobronchial tree contains no aspirated material or blood. Multiple sections of the lungs show congestion and edematous fluid exuding from the cut surface. No consolidation or suppuration is noted. The mucosa of the larynx is grayish white.

Liver and biliary system: The liver weighs 1890 grams. The surface is dark brown and smooth. There are marked adhesions through the omentum and abdominal wall in the lower portion of the liver as the gallbladder has been removed. The common duct is widely patent. No calculus or obstructive material is found. Multiple sections of the liver show slight accentuation of the lobular pattern; however, no hemorrhage or tumor is found.

Hemic and lymphatic system: The spleen weighs 190 grams. The surface is dark red and smooth. Section shows dark red homogeneous firm cut surface. The Malpighian bodies are not clearly identified. There is no evidence of lymphadenopathy. The bone marrow is dark red in color. Endocrine system: The adrenal glands have the usual architectural cortex and medulla. The thyroid glands are of normal size, color and consistency. Urinary system: The kidneys together weigh 350 grams. Their capsules can be stripped without difficulty. Dissection shows a moderately congested parenchyma. The cortical surface is smooth. The pelves and ureters are not dilated or stenosed. The urinary bladder contains approximately 150 cc. of clear straw-colored fluid. The mucosa is not altered.

Genital system: The external genitalia shows no gross

abnormality. Distribution of the pubic hair is of female pattern. The uterus is of the usual size. Multiple sections of the uterus show the usual thickness of the uterine wall without tumor nodules. The endometrium is grayish yellow, measuring up to 0.2 cm in thickness. No polyp or tumor is found. The cervix is clear, showing no nabothian cysts. The tubes are intact. The right ovary demonstrates recent corpus luteum haemorrhagicum. The left ovary shows corpora lutea and albicantia. A vaginal smear is taken.

Digestive system: The esophagus has a longitudinal folding mucosa. The stomach is almost completely empty. The contents is brownish mucoid fluid. The volume is estimated to be no more than 20 cc. No residue of the pills is noted. A smear made from the gastric contents and examined under the polarized microscope shows no refractile crystals. The mucosa shows marked congestion and submucosal petechial hemorrhage diffusely. The duodenum shows no ulcer. The contents of the duodenum is also examined under polarized microscope and shows no refractile crystals. The remainder of the small intestine shows no gross abnormality. The appendix is absent. The colon shows marked congestion and purplish discoloration. The pancreas has a tan lobular architecture. Multiple sections shows a patent duct.

Skeletomuscular system: The clavicle, ribs, vertebrae and pelvic bones show fracture lines. All bones of the extremities are examined by palpation showing no evidence of fracture.

Head and central nervous system: The brain weighs 1440 grams. Upon reflection of the scalp there is no evidence of contusion or hemorrhage. The temporal muscles are intact. Upon removal of the dura mater the cerebrospinal fluid is clear. The superficial vessels are slightly congested. The convolutions of the brain are not flattened. The contour of the brain is not distorted. No blood is found in the epidural, subdural or subarachnoid spaces. Multiple sections of the brain show the usual symmetrical ventricles and basal ganglia. Examination of the cerebellum and brain stem shows no gross abnormality. Following removal of the dura mater from the base of the skull and calvarium no skull fracture is demonstrated.

Liver temperature taken at 10:30 A.M. registered 89 F

Specimen: Unembalmed blood is taken for alcohol and barbiturate examination. Liver, kidney, stomach and contents, urine and intestine are saved for further toxicological study. A vaginal smear is made. - *T NOGUCHI, M.D. DEPUTY MEDICAL EXAMINER 8-13-62*

Investigations into Her Death:

There was a review of Marilyn's death in 1982. The findings were published December 28, 1982. In the 1982 inquest, District Attorney John Van de Kamp said that Marilyn Monroe's death could have been a suicide or an accidental drug overdose, and that no further inquiry was planned.

The 29-page report found that there was no credible evidence to support any murder theory.

Follow-up:

At a news conference on October 28, 1985, after resigning as foreman of the Los Angeles County grand jury, Sam Cordova called for yet another new investigation into the death of Marilyn Monroe, due to many unresolved questions. District Attorney Ira Reiner stated that there was no need for a new investigation. Cordova then called for the appointment of a special state prosecutor to investigate her death. In late August of 1992, Los Angeles County Supervisor Michael D. Antonovich unsuccessfully sought to reopen the investigation into Marilyn Monroe's death in order to investigate discrepancies.

The Funeral:

Statement to the Press and to the World

We sincerely hope that the many friends of Marilyn will understand that we are deeply appreciative of their desire to pay last respects to Marilyn whom we all loved. We hope that each person will understand that last rites must of great necessity be as private as possible so that she can go on to her final resting place in the quiet she always sought. We could not in conscience ask one personality to attend without perhaps offending many, many others and for this reason alone, we have kept the number of persons to a minimum. Please...all of you...remember the gay, sweet Marilyn and say a prayer of farewell within the confines of your home or your church.

- Berniece Miracle, Inez Melson, Joe DiMaggio

The private service was conducted by A.J. Soldan, a

Lutheran minister from the Village Church of Westwood.

Monroe was buried in an $800 coffin on August 8, 1962, reportedly the day that Joe and Marilyn were to be remarried. (NOTE: $800 spent in 1962 would equal almost $6,000 today.)

The 25 or so invited attendees at the small service included Joe DiMaggio, Joe DiMaggio, Jr., Marilyn's half-sister, Berniece Baker Miracle, Lee and Paula Strasberg, Inez Melson, Dr. Greenson and his family, Sydney Guilaroff, Allan "Whitey" Snyder, Pat Newcomb, Marilyn's publicist, Eunice Murray, Marilyn's housekeeper, and Marilyn's secretary, attorneys, driver, maid and hairdressers.

Also reported to have been invited but not attending were Marilyn's former husbands, James Dougherty and Arthur Miller. Marilyn's mother, Gladys, was in a sanitarium and was never informed of her death. She outlived Marilyn another 22 years.

The hearse was a 1962 Cadillac Eureka Landau funeral coach. There were four pallbearers: Two of the four were Allan Abbott and Ron Hast of Abbott & Hast, the company that arranged the funeral and provided the funeral car. The other two were Sydney Guilaroff, the esteemed Emmy-award-winning hair stylist (the first hair stylist ever listed in film credits), whom a distraught Marilyn called on the phone the night before she died, and Allan "Whitey" Snyder, Marilyn's personal make-up artist from the time of her first screen test at Twentieth Century Fox in 1946 through all of her films. Toward the end of her life, Marilyn asked Snyder to prepare her face if she were to die before him, a promise he kept by applying her makeup in preparation for the funeral.

The Eulogy:

Monroe's former acting coach, mentor, friend and beneficiary, Lee Strasberg, delivered the eulogy (it has been said that Joe first asked Carl Sandberg to deliver the eulogy, but he declined due to ill health). The full text of the eulogy appears below. The song played during the service was Judy Garland's "Over the Rainbow," said to be one of Marilyn's personal favorites.

Lee Strasberg's Eulogy

Marilyn Monroe was a legend.

In her own lifetime she created a myth of what a poor girl from a deprived background could attain. For the entire world she became a symbol of the eternal feminine.

But I have no words to describe the myth and the legend. I did not know this Marilyn Monroe. We gathered here today, knew only Marilyn—a warm human being, impulsive and shy, sensitive and in fear of rejection, yet ever avid for life and reaching out for fulfillment. I will not insult the privacy of your memory of her—a privacy she sought and treasured—by trying to describe her whom you knew to you who knew her. In our memories of her she remains alive, not only a shadow on the screen or a glamorous personality.

For us Marilyn was a devoted and loyal

friend, a colleague constantly reaching for perfection. We shared her pain and difficulties and some of her joys. She was a member of our family. It is difficult to accept the fact that her zest for life has been ended by this dreadful accident.

Despite the heights and brilliance she attained on the screen, she was planning for the future; she was looking forward to participating in the many exciting things which she planned. In her eyes and in mine her career was just beginning.

The dream of her talent, which she had nurtured as a child, was not a mirage. When she first came to me I was amazed at the startling sensitivity which she possessed and which had remained fresh and undimmed, struggling to express itself despite the life to which she had been subjected.

Others were as physically beautiful as she was, but there was obviously something more in her, something that people saw and recognized in her performances and with which they identified. She had a luminous quality—a combination of wistfulness, radiance, yearning—to set her apart and yet make everyone wish to be a part of it, to share in the childish naïveté which was so shy and yet so vibrant.

This quality was even more evident when she was on the stage. I am truly sorry that the public who loved her did not have the opportunity to see her as we did, in many of the roles that foreshadowed what she would have become.

Without a doubt she would have been one of the really great actresses of the stage.

Now it is at an end. I hope her death will stir sympathy and understanding for a sensitive artist and a woman who brought joy and pleasure to the world.

I cannot say goodbye. Marilyn never liked goodbyes, but in the peculiar way she had of turning things around so that they faced reality—I will say *au revoir*. For the country to which she has gone, we must all someday visit.

The Interment:

Marilyn was laid to rest on August 8, 1962, at Westwood Memorial Park's "Corridor of Memories" in Los Angeles. Thousands of fans lined the streets to grieve for the legendary Marilyn Monroe.

Following her death, Hugh Hefner purchased the crypt next to Marilyn, reportedly paying $85,000. NOTE: $85,000 in 1962 would equate to more than $612,000 in 2010.

In August of 2009 a $4.6 million eBay bid fell through for the purchase of the crypt above Marilyn's.

Westwood Memorial Park:

Every day an estimated 300 people visit Marilyn Monroe's aboveground crypt in Westwood Village Memorial Park, just off the UCLA campus in Westwood. The marble has been darkened by the touch of so many hands, and cemetery employees must repeatedly remove the lipstick marks left by

Marilyn's fans.

A few feet in front of Marilyn's crypt is a white stone bench, which was paid for and installed in 1992, on the 30th anniversary of her death, by two Monroe fan clubs, All About Marilyn and Marilyn Remembered.

In 2008 the Marilyn Remembered fan club invited fans worldwide to contribute funds in order to replace the crumbling bench. In February of 2009 a new bench was installed, thanks to their donations.

Every year on the anniversary of her death, the Marilyn Remembered fan club hosts a memorial service at Westwood, usually attracting hundreds of friends, fans, impersonators and dozens of floral arrangements in front of her crypt.

Other celebrities buried in Westwood are Jack Lemmon, Billy Wilder, Dean Martin, Natalie Wood, Carroll O'Connor, Truman Capote, Bob Crane, Farrah Fawcett, Rodney Dangerfield, and actresses Dominique Dunne and Heather O'Rourke from the film *Poltergeist*.

The Legend of the Roses:

Just as William Powell had reputedly done for Jean Harlow, Joe DiMaggio arranged for roses to be delivered to Marilyn's grave for years after her death. It is widely believed that the roses were delivered to her grave twice a week for twenty years, possibly stopping after Joe moved to Florida or —as some report—because the roses were almost always stolen.

HELLO, NORMA JEAN

Joe DiMaggio's Last Words:

Morris Engelberg, Joe DiMaggio's attorney, is quoted as saying that Joe's final words were, "I'll finally get to see Marilyn." On the other hand, a hospice worker told the *New York Daily News* that DiMaggio had no last words.

Jean Harlow and Marilyn Similarities:

There are a number of interesting parallels in the lives of Marilyn Monroe and Jean Harlow: Both were raised as Christian Scientists, Marilyn for eight years (later in life she would convert to Judaism before marrying Arthur Miller); both married at 16 and had 3 marriages; both were blonde bombshells in the movies; and both starred with Clark Gable in their last movies.

Comments After Her Death:

"She could have made it with a little luck."
Arthur Miller

"The awful last headline: Marilyn Monroe Dead of Overdose of Pills. Why do things happen this way, my dear?"
Louella Parsons
gossip columnist

"She was pure of heart. She was free of guile. She never understood either the adoration or the antagonism which she awakened."

Edward Wagenknecht
author, literary critic and teacher

"She stood for life. She radiated life. In her smile hope was always present. She glorified in life, and her death did not mar this final image. She had become a legend in her own time, and in her death, took her place among the myths of our century."

John Kobal
author and film historian

"This atrocious death will be a terrible lesson for those whose principal occupation consists in spying on and tormenting the film stars."

Jean Cocteau
novelist, playwright, director,
poet, painter and actor

"Anyone who has ever felt resentment against the good for being the good, and has given voice to it, is the murderer of Marilyn Monroe."

Ayn Rand
novelist and philosopher

"She will go on eternally."

Jackie Kennedy Onassis

"In one sense, then, her life is completed, because her spirit is formed and has achieved itself. No matter what unpredictable events may be in her future, they cannot change who she is and what she has become."

Maurice Zolotow
biographer

"Gosh there were a lot of people who loved her. She had loyal fans. There were no pretenses about Marilyn Monroe.

"I had great respect for her as an artist and as a person. She was a lovely girl. She had a great mind. The girl's got character. The first sixteen years of her life was enough to floor most of us. She never fully realized herself. The best years for her were ahead of her, the best years were the years to come."

Carl Sandburg
Pulitzer Prize winning author and poet

"She seemed to have a kind of unconscious glow about her physical self that was innocent, like a child."

Elizabeth Taylor

"I know people who say 'Hollywood broke her heart,' and all that, but I don't believe it. She was very observant and tough minded and appealing, but she adored and trusted the wrong people."

George Cukor
director

"Do you remember when Marilyn Monroe died? Everybody stopped work, and you could see all that day the same expressions on their faces, the same thought: 'How can a girl with success, fame, youth, money, beauty … how could she kill herself?' Nobody could understand it because those are the things that everybody wants, and they can't believe that life wasn't important to Marilyn Monroe, or that her life was elsewhere."

Marlon Brando

"It's difficult to say what Marilyn's future would have been, but I believe her career would have continued, and she would have been an important actress. I never worked with her, but I think some of the people who did failed to give her the patience and consideration she needed. She had her problems. She was disturbed in many areas, and those who weren't close friends of hers may not have realized how grave some of her personal problems were."

Peter Lawford

"She was so lovely and too young to die. God bless her...I never met Marilyn Monroe, but if I had, I would have tried very hard to help her...A sex symbol is a heavy load to carry when one is tired, hurt, and bewildered."

Clara Bow,
actress/The 'It' Girl

"We were very close. Once when we were doing that picture together, I got a call on the set: my younger daughter had had a fall. I ran home and the one person to call was Marilyn. She did an awful lot to boost things up for movies when everything was at a low state; there'll never be anyone like her for looks, for attitude, for all of it."

Betty Grable

"If you knew every last detail of Marilyn's death, you still wouldn't know any more about her...who she was or the mysteries of the human heart, which were the things she was interested in."

Susan Strasberg
actress and author,
daughter of Lee and Paula Strasberg

"Marilyn was the quintessential victim of the male and also of her own self-destroying perversities."

Hedda Rosten
writer

"She was a difficult woman, you know. We liked her and we said the nicest things about her and she deserved them; but, she was trouble and she brought that whole baggage of emotional difficulties of her childhood with her."

Norman Rosten
poet and playwright

"I have great faith that her career would have continued. She was one of the greatest draws in the history of motion pictures, and today I think she would have been tops. Marilyn had a childlike quality which made men adore her. Yet women weren't jealous. Like John Wayne and a few other giants, she had a star quality that had nothing to do with acting... What women in pictures can compare with her today? Nobody."

Ben Lyon
Twentieth Century Fox studio executive and actor

"Unique is an overworked word, but in her case it applies. There will never be another one like her, and Lord knows there have been plenty of imitations."

Billy Wilder
director

"I knew Marilyn and I loved her dearly. She asked me for help—ME! I didn't know what to tell her. One night at a party at Clifton Webb's house Marilyn followed me from room to room. 'I don't want to get too far away from you, I'm scared,' she said. I told her 'We're all scared. I'm scared too."

Judy Garland

"Marilyn Monroe's unique charisma was the force that caused distant men to think that if only a well-intentioned, understanding person like me could have known her, she would have been all right. In death, it has caused women who before resented her frolicsome sexuality to join in the unspoken plea she leaves behind—the simple, noble wish to be taken seriously."

Time magazine

"Her death has diminished the loveliness of the world in which we live."

Life magazine

"Marilyn Monroe...the most fragile and loveable legend of all."

Look magazine

The Will:

The following is a plain-language summary of the provisions of Marilyn's will. The complete will is set forth following the summary.

To Bernice Miracle, Marilyn's half-sister, $10,000;

To May Reis, her assistant/secretary, $10,000;

To Norman and Hedda Rosten, friends of Marilyn and Arthur Miller, $5,000 toward the education of their daughter,

Patricia;

To a trust, $100,000 for the following purposes:

For Gladys Baker, Marilyn's mother, $5,000 per year;

For Xenia Chekhov, widow of Marilyn's early acting coach, Michael Chekhov, $2,500 per year;

Following the deaths of Gladys Baker and Xenia Chekhov, the remaining balance of the trust to be paid to Dr. Marianne Kris (Marilyn's psychiatrist in NY), to be donated to the psychiatric institution of her choice (Dr. Kris donated her inheritance to Hampstead Child Therapy Clinic in London);

The remainder of her estate to be divided as follows:

To May Reis, $40,000 or 25% of the total remainder of the trust (whichever is less);

To Dr. Marianne Kris, 25% of the balance for the same purposes as the bequest of the remainder of the trust above;

To Lee Strasberg, her acting coach and mentor, 50% of the balance, and all of her personal effects and clothing to be distributed, at his discretion, to her friends and colleagues.

Last Will and Testament of Marilyn Monroe

I, MARILYN MONROE, do make, publish and declare this to be my Last Will and Testament.

FIRST: I hereby revoke all former Wills and Codicils by me made.

SECOND: I direct my Executor, hereinafter named, to pay all of my just debts, funeral expenses and testamentary charges as soon after my death as can conveniently be done.

THIRD: I direct that all succession, estate or inheritance taxes which may be levied against my estate and/or against any legacies and/or devises hereinafter set forth shall be paid out of my residuary estate.

FOURTH: (a) I give and bequeath to BERNICE MIRACLE, should she survive me, the sum of $10,000.00.

(b) I give and bequeath to MAY REIS, should she survive me, the sum of $10,000.00.

(c) I give and bequeath to NORMAN and HEDDA ROSTEN, or to the survivor of them, or if they should both predecease me, then to their daughter, PATRICIA ROSTEN, the sum of $5,000.00, it being my wish that such sum be used for the education of PATRICIA ROSTEN.

(d) I give and bequeath all of my personal effects and clothing to LEE STRASBERG, or if he should predecease me, then to my Executor hereinafter named, it being my desire that he distribute these, in his sole discretion, among my friends, colleagues and those to whom I am devoted.

FIFTH; I give and bequeath to my Trustee, hereinafter named, the sum of $100,000.00, in Trust, for the following uses and purposes:

(a) To hold, manage, invest and reinvest the said property and to receive and collect the income therefrom.

(b) To pay the net income therefrom, together with such amounts of principal as shall be necessary to provide $5,000.00 per annum, in equal quarterly installments, for the maintenance and support of my mother, GLADYS BAKER, during her lifetime.

(c) To pay the net income therefrom, together with such amounts of principal as shall be necessary to provide $2,500.00 per annum, in equal quarterly installments, for the maintenance and support of MRS. MICHAEL CHEKHOV during her lifetime.

(d) Upon the death of the survivor between my mother,

GLADYS BAKER, and MRS. MICHAEL CHEKHOV to pay over the principal remaining in the Trust, together with any accumulated income, to DR. MARIANNE KRIS to be used by her for the furtherance of the work of such psychiatric institutions or groups as she shall elect.

SIXTH: All the rest, residue and remainder of my estate, both real and personal, of whatsoever nature and wheresoever situate, of which I shall die seized or possessed or to which I shall be in any way entitled, or over which I shall possess any power of appointment by Will at the time of my death, including any lapsed legacies, I give, devise and bequeath as follows:

(a) To MAY REIS the sum of $40,000.00 or 25% of the total remainder of my estate, whichever shall be the lesser,

(b) To DR. MARIANNE KRIS 25% of the balance thereof, to be used by her as set forth in ARTICLE FIFTH (d) of this my Last Will and Testament.

(c) To LEE STRASBERG the entire remaining balance.

SEVENTH: I nominate, constitute and appoint AARON R. FROSCH Executor of this my Last Will and Testament. In the event that he should die or fail to qualify, or resign or for any other reason be unable to act, I nominate, constitute and appoint L. ARNOLD WEISSBERGER in his place and stead.

EIGHTH: I nominate, constitute and appoint AARON R. FROSCH Trustee under this my Last Will and Testament. In the event he should die or fail to qualify, or resign or for any other reason be unable to act, I nominate, constitute and appoint L. Arnold Weissberger in his place and stead.

Marilyn Monroe (L.S.)

SIGNED, SEALED, PUBLISHED and DECLARED by MARILYN MONROE, the Testatrix above named, as and for her Last Will and Testament, in our presence and we, at her request and in her presence and in the presence of each other, have hereunto subscribed our names as witnesses this 14th day of January, One Thousand Nine Hundred Sixty-One

Aaron R. Frosch residing at 10 West 86th St. NYC

Louise H. White residing at 709 E. 56 St., New York, NY

Her Estate:

Marilyn left an estate valued at $1.6 million. The licensing of Marilyn's name and likeness, handled worldwide by Curtis Management Group, reportedly nets the Monroe estate about $2 million per year.

Controversies:

Her will was filed in August of 1962, and in October it was contested by Inez Melson, Marilyn's business manager. She claimed that either Lee Strasberg or Dr. Kris had influenced Marilyn. The judge ruled against Ms. Melson and the will was probated.

At his discretion, as allowed by Marilyn's will, Lee Strasberg never sold or gave away any of Marilyn's personal effects (furniture, clothing, etc.). Upon Lee's death in 1982, his second wife, Anna (his first wife, Paula, Marilyn's acting coach, had died in 1966), inherited all of Marilyn's belongings. It is thought that the royalties and licensing from Marilyn's image reportedly brings in $2 million per year. In late 1999, Christie's auction of Marilyn's personal items netted over $12 million dollars.

Conspiracy Theories:

In 1972, actress Veronica Hamel, known for her starring role on *Hill Street Blues,* and her husband bought Marilyn's Brentwood, California home. During the remodel, their contractor discovered an eavesdropping system throughout the home. These sophisticated components were not commercially available in 1962. A retired Justice Department official called them "standard FBI issue." This discovery lent further support to the belief of conspiracy theorists that Marilyn had been under surveillance by the Kennedys and possibly the Mafia.

There have been persistent claims that Marilyn had affairs with John and/or Robert Kennedy. Rumors surfaced that Kennedy brother-in-law, actor Peter Lawford, thought that Marilyn had totally unrealistic notions about becoming First Lady and that her letters and telephone calls to both JFK and RFK had become troublesome. Marilyn was aware of Kennedy private matters and could prove dangerous to their political careers.

There were implications that Jack and/or Bobby Kennedy had told Marilyn far too much about Roswell and UFOs, and could have put the nation's reputation in jeopardy.

Did Robert Kennedy bring Marilyn the news of his brother's desire to break off his relationship on the night Marilyn died? Did he come to her home to break off their own affair? A Beverly Hills police officer reportedly stopped a Mercedes speeding past the house on the night of Marilyn's death. In the car were Bobby Kennedy, Peter Lawford and Marilyn's psychiatrist. A neighbor of Marilyn's was quoted as seeing Robert Kennedy walk into the Monroe home with two other men that night. In the memoirs of former Los Angeles

Police Chief, Daryl Gates, who died April 16, 2010, at age 83, he stated that the Police Department knew that Robert Kennedy was in Los Angeles on August 4, 1962.

Marilyn Monroe's FBI File:

The FBI file on Marilyn Monroe was released in 2006 under the Freedom of Information Act. The portion that is available online consists of two parts containing a total of more than 100 pages and can be viewed at http://foia.fbi.gov/foiaindex/monroe.htm. Many of the documents have been redacted—that is, names, places, dates and other information deemed by the FBI to be sensitive have been blacked out.

Was there an attempt by the U.S. Government to cover up JFK's (and/or RFK's) indiscretions with Marilyn? The alleged cover-up was believed to have extended beyond the phone records and police evidence found at the scene.

Shortly after 11:00 PM on the night of Marilyn's death, it is believed that Peter Lawford and Pat Newcomb, Marilyn's former secretary and press agent, went to Marilyn's house. Purportedly, Lawford called Bobby Kennedy and explained what had occurred.

The FBI file contains a memo dated July 9, 1963, from a Mr. M. A. Jones to a Mr. DeLoach discussing and summarizing an article by columnist Walter Winchell that appeared in the July 8, 1963, issue of the *New York Mirror*, in which Marilyn is alleged to have been murdered by a man with whom Marilyn had an affair—a man who was "a great man, famous, known the world over," who "can be seen on television and in movie theaters," and who is "mentioned almost daily in newspapers and magazines." The memo appears after the report on Robert F. Kennedy.

Another theory is that Marilyn was murdered by the Mafia, eager to avenge itself on the Kennedys for RFK's vendetta against them. Yet another theory involved the fact that one or both of the Kennedy brothers had shared information with Marilyn about a possible assassination attempt on Fidel Castro.

Dorothy Kilgallen, investigative reporter and known to most as a panelist on the popular game show *What's My Line?* was the first to write about Marilyn's questionable suicide and the discrepancies in the official story of JFK's murder. In late 1965, she also interviewed Jack Ruby, who shot and killed JFK assassin, Lee Harvey Oswald. Kilgallen had announced that she was going to reveal the *real* story about President Kennedy's murder, questioning the Warren Commission's lone gunman, single bullet determination. On the morning of November 8, 1965, Dorothy Kilgallen was found dead. She was sitting upright in bed and fully dressed. Supposedly all her notes on the JFK assassination had disappeared.

Commemoratives:

Marilyn Monroe's star was placed at 6774 Hollywood Boulevard on February 9, 1960.

Marilyn Monroe's United States Postal Service 32¢ stamp in the Legends of Hollywood series was issued June 1, 1995. The Marilyn Monroe's stamp was the BEST-SELLING single postage stamp of 1995, with 46.3 million sold.

Awards:

"Miss California Artichoke Queen," 1947

"The Present That All GIs Would Like to Find in Their Christmas Stocking," 1951

"The Best Young Box Office Personality," *The Henrietta Awards*, 1951

"Cheesecake Queen of 1952," *Stars and Stripes*, 1952

"Fastest Rising Star of 1952," *Photoplay* magazine, 1952

"Most Promising Female Newcomer," *Look* magazine, 1952

"The Most Advertised Girl in the World," Advertising Association of the West, 1953

"Best Young Box Office Personality," *Redbook* magazine, 1953

"World Film Favorite," the Golden Globe® Awards, 1953

"Best Actress," *Photoplay* magazine, 1954, for *Gentlemen Prefer Blondes* and *How to Marry a Millionaire*

"Best Foreign Actress," the *David Di Donatello Prize* (Italian Oscar), for *The Prince and the Showgirl*, 1958

"Best Foreign Actress," 1959, the *Crystal Star Award* (French Oscar) for *The Prince and the Showgirl*, 1959

"Best Actress in a Comedy," the Golden Globe® Awards for *Some Like It Hot*, 1959

"World Film Favorite," the Golden Globe® Awards, 1961

"Sexiest Female Movie Star of All Time," UK's *Empire Magazine*, 1995

"Sexiest Woman of the Century," *People* magazine, 1999

"Number One Sex Star of the 20th Century," by *Playboy* magazine, 1999

"Sixth Greatest Female Star of All Time," American Film Institute, 1999

NOTE: Marilyn was never nominated for an Academy Award. In February 2010 *Entertainment Weekly* magazine listed Marilyn as Number 1 among the Top 20 of those Never Nominated, including, among others, Christian Bale, Myrna Loy, Gary Oldman, Joseph Cotten, Errol Flynn, Dennis Quaid, and Kim Novak.

Select Photographers:

Andre de Dienes: In 1945 fashion photographer Andre de Dienes met Norma Jean Dougherty. It's rumored that he and Norma Jean were briefly engaged. Andre captured Norma Jean in countless photographs in natural settings, helping to launch her modeling career.

Milton H. Greene: On assignment for *Look* magazine, Milton first met Marilyn and they became close friends. They became business partners when forming Marilyn Monroe Productions, a film production company that produced *Bus Stop* and *The Prince and the Showgirl*. Before marrying Arthur Miller, Marilyn lived with Milton and his family in Connecticut. During their enduring friendship, Milton Greene captured some of her most memorable photographs. Marilyn's "Ballerina" image in the loose-fitting white satin and tulle dress was photographed by Milton in 1954. This often reproduced photo was chosen as one of *Time-Life*'s three most popular images of the 20th Century. The other two were photographs of Albert Einstein by Phillipe Halsman and Yousuf Karsh's photograph of Winston Churchill.

Bert Stern: On assignment for *Vogue*, Bert Stern shot Marilyn's last photo session six weeks before her death. Some 2,500 shots were taken over a 3-day sitting. NOTE: On

December 16, 2008, Christie's New York sold 36 photos of Marilyn Monroe from Bert Stern's *The Last Sitting*. Each gelatin silver print was signed, dated and numbered. The collection sold for $146,500.

Richard Avedon: In April 2008 famed photographer Richard Avedon's photograph of Marilyn Monroe, entitled "Marilyn Monroe, Actress, New York City, May 6, 1957," was sold at Sotheby's auction in New York for $457,000. This famous photo was of Marilyn in a halter style sequined dress with the characteristically low-cut deep V neckline, but without her characteristic smile. Instead, Marilyn looks detached, deep in thought.

Alfred Eisenstaedt: In 1953 Alfred Eisenstaedt (known as "Eisie") photographed Marilyn for *LIFE* magazine. His famous shots taken on her Hollywood patio are of Marilyn in a simple black turtleneck and slacks.

Sir Cecil Beaton: Of the countless photographs taken of Marilyn, her supposed personal favorite is an ethereal shot taken by acclaimed fashion and portrait photographer, Sir Cecil Beaton. In the photograph, Marilyn is reclining in a white gauzy dress and clutches a long-stemmed flower against her chest. This photo was said to have been displayed in her New York apartment.

Beaton was a former staff photographer for *Vanity Fair* and *Vogue*, who often photographed the Royal Family. For costume design, he won four Tony Awards. His two Academy Awards for Costume Design were for *Gigi* and *My Fair Lady*.

HELLO, NORMA JEAN

Ultimate Hollywood Beauties:

As recently as February of 2009, Marilyn made the Top Five as *Marie Claire Magazine* readers voted on the Ultimate Hollywood Beauties:

1 Audrey Hepburn
2 Angelina Jolie
3 Grace Kelly
4 Marilyn Monroe
5 Sophia Loren
6 Catherine Zeta-Jones
7 Elizabeth Taylor
8 Keira Knightley
9 Halle Berry
10 Brigitte Bardot
11 Julia Roberts
12 Vivien Leigh
13 Nicole Kidman
14 Cameron Diaz
15 Doris Day
16 Scarlett Johansson
17 Charlize Theron
18 Jennifer Aniston
19 Michelle Pfeiffer
20 Liv Tyler

Red Hot Lovers:

February 2009, LA *Entertainment Examiner*'s Top 10 Hollywood red hot lovers:

Number 1—Brad Pitt and Angelina Jolie

Number 2—Elizabeth Taylor and Richard Burton
Number 3—Humphrey Bogart and Lauren Bacall
Number 4—Katherine Hepburn and Spencer Tracy
Number 5—Clark Gable and Carole Lombard
Number 6—Marilyn Monroe and Joe DiMaggio
NOTE: Joe was in her life until her death.

Filmography:

1947 - *The Shocking Miss Pilgrim* (uncredited role)

1947 - *Dangerous Years*

1948 - *You Were Meant For Me* (uncredited role)

1948 - *Scudda Hoo! Scudda Hay!* (uncredited role)

1948 - *Green Grass of Wyoming* (uncredited role)

1948 - *Ladies of the Chorus*

1949 - *Love Happy* (uncredited role)

1950 - *A Ticket to Tomahawk* (uncredited role)

1950 - *Right Cross* (uncredited role)

1950 - *The Fireball*

1950 - *The Asphalt Jungle*

1950 - *All About Eve*

1951 - *Love Nest*

1951 - *Let's Make It Legal*

1951 - *Home Town Story*

1951 - *As Young as You Feel*

1952 - *O. Henry's Full House*

1952 - *Monkey Business*

1952 - *Clash by Night*

1952 - *We're Not Married!*

1952 - *Don't Bother to Knock*

1953 - *Niagara*

1953 - *Gentlemen Prefer Blondes*
1953 - *How to Marry a Millionaire*
1954 - *River of No Return*
1954 - *There's No Business Like Show Business*
1955 - *The Seven Year Itch*
1956 - *Bus Stop*
1957 - *The Prince and the Showgirl*
1959 - *Some Like It Hot*
1960 - *Let's Make Love*
1961 - *The Misfits*
1962 - *Something's Got to Give* (unfinished)

Approval of Directors:

In September of 1955, after Marilyn's enormously successful film, *The Seven Year Itch*, Twentieth Century Fox agreed to her unprecedented (for the time) contract demands, including story, cinematographer and director approval.

Her Last Movie:

Marilyn worked only 12 of the 31 shooting days on the movie, *Something's Got to Give*. After Marilyn was fired from the movie, co-star Dean Martin exercised a clause in his contract that gave him approval over the choice of his leading lady. He insisted that Marilyn be re-hired to finish the film. She was reinstated but died before filming could resume.

NOTES:
• In 2001 on what would have been Marilyn's 75th birthday, American Movie Classics aired 37 minutes of never-

before-seen footage from *Something's Got to Give*.

    • *Something's Got to Give* was remade in 1963's *Move Over, Darling* with Doris Day and James Garner in the lead roles. Many of the existing sets from the Marilyn Monroe/Dean Martin movie were used. Coincidentally, *Something's Got to Give* was itself a remake of the 1940 Cary Grant/Irene Dunne comedy, *My Favorite Wife*.

Favorable Movie Reviews:

    • *Some Like It Hot:* Review of *Some Like It Hot* by A.H. Weiler in the esteemed *New York Times*, published March 30, 1959:

    "...Miss Monroe, whose figure simply cannot be overlooked, contributes more assets than the obvious ones to this madcap romp.

    "...proves to be the epitome of a dumb blonde and a talented comedienne."

    NOTE: In September 2009 the Hotel del Coronado in San Diego County—the location for filming *Some Like It Hot*—celebrated the 50th anniversary of the filming. The film was voted the "Number One Comedy of All Time" by the American Film Institute. Their special guest was legendary actor, Tony Curtis, who starred in the movie with Marilyn.

    NOTE: It's hard to imagine anyone other than Marilyn Monroe playing Sugar, but it was said that Billy Wilder's first choice to play the role was Mitzi Gaynor. Wilder reportedly offered Frank Sinatra the role of Jerry/Daphne (played in the movie by Tony Curtis) as his first choice.

• *Niagara:* In a less-than-stellar review of *Niagara* by A.H. Weiler, published in the *New York Times* on January 22, 1953, Marilyn garnered some praise:

"...the grandeur that is Marilyn Monroe."

"...they have illustrated pretty concretely that she can be seductive—even when she walks."

"...the falls and Miss Monroe are something to see."

• *Gentlemen Prefer Blondes:* In Bosley Crowthers' *New York Times* review of *Gentlemen Prefer Blondes*, published July 16, 1953, he found fault with the script and direction, but praised Marilyn and co-star, Jane Russell:

"...Miss Russell and Miss Monroe keep you looking at them even when they have little or nothing to do. Call it inherent magnetism. Call it luxurious coquetry. Call it whatever you fancy. It's what makes this a—well, a buoyant show."

Dubious Film Ratings:

• *Gentlemen Prefer Blondes*, named "One of the Ten Worst Films of the Year" by the *Harvard Lampoon*, 1953
• *How to Marry a Millionaire*, named "One of the Ten Worst Films of the Year" by the *Harvard Lampoon*, 1953

• *There's No Business Like Show Business,* named "One of the Ten Worst Films of the Year" by the *Harvard Lampoon,* 1954

Auctions:

Christie's Auction: On October 27 and 28, 1999, Christie's conducted an auction of numerous items of Marilyn Monroe memorabilia that were owned by the widow of Lee Strasberg, Marilyn's acting coach. The prices obtained for more than 150 items totaled $13,405,785. The "Happy Birthday, Mister President" gown was sold for a record-shattering $1,267,500.00. This is the highest price ever paid for a piece of clothing, is in the *Guinness Book of World Records*, and remains the record as of this writing (July 2010). The previous record was $250,000 paid for one of Princess Diana's gowns in 1997. In June of 2010, the black taffeta dress worn by Princess Diana at her first official appearance with Prince Charles after announcing their engagement sold in London at auction for $276,000, still far below the record set with Marilyn's "Happy Birthday, Mister President" gown.

More Results from the Christie's Auction:

• The diamond and platinum eternity ring that DiMaggio gave to Monroe was sold for $772,500.
• A pair of earrings brought in $35,000; a pair of red heels earned $48,300; a bidder paid $21,000 for a floor lamp; the *Some Like It Hot* script brought in $51,750; one of her *Golden Globe*® awards was auctioned off for $140,000; and *The Misfits* script went for $31,000.

• Tommy Hilfiger reportedly paid $42,000 for the jeans that Marilyn wore in *River of No Return* and $75,000 for the boots she wore in *The Misfits*.

• Singer Mariah Carey revealed in April 2006 that she paid $662,500 at the auction for Marilyn's white baby grand piano.

Julien's Auctions: Among the many items sold at Julien's $1 million auction in June of 2005:

• Marilyn's original watercolor of a single red rose inscribed to President John F. Kennedy, reading "Happy Birthday President Kennedy from Marilyn Monroe," June 1, 1962 (with a Christie's sticker as it was originally intended to be sold there in 1999)—starting bid, $4,000, final bid, $78,000.

• Marilyn's cotton sleeveless sundress with decorative trim around the neck and arms (stained with a broken zipper and frayed eyelet trim—but it was photographed when she and Arthur Miller were in New York in 1956, and the item included an image of Marilyn wearing this dress): the starting bid was $2,000, the final bid, $21,000.

• Marilyn's black wool dress with spaghetti straps— starting bid, $300, final bid, $19,200.

• Marilyn's black wool knee-length sweater from Saks Fifth Avenue—starting bid, $100, final bid, $12,600.

• Marilyn's black strapless underwire bra (had a Christie's tag pinned to it as it was originally scheduled to be sold there in 1999)—starting bid, $50, final bid, $5,700.

• Marilyn's 1958 Screen Actors Guild membership card —starting bid was $500, final bid, $4,200.

• Marilyn's savings account book with deposits and withdrawals from February of 1956 through January of 1962—starting bid, $350, final bid, $1,200.

• Marilyn's 6-1/2" long gold mesh wallet with pink satin lining—starting bid, $500, final bid, $6,000.

• Marilyn's Oster blender—starting bid, $350, final bid, $1,440.

• Marilyn's October 1952 $300 personal check written to her acting coach, Natasha Lytess—starting bid, $300, final bid, $2,880.

Julien's Auction at the Planet Hollywood Resort and Casino in Las Vegas, Late June 2009: Among items from Marilyn, Michael Jackson and Elvis, the item with the highest winning bid was the white hooded terry cloth robe Marilyn wore during her beach photo shoot captured by noted photographer George Barris. This short robe sold for $120,000.

Julien's Auction held in late June 2010 at the Planet Hollywood Resort and Casino in Las Vegas:

• A 1954 chest x-ray from 28-year-old Marilyn Monroe, taken at Cedars of Lebanon Hospital (now Cedars–Sinai Medical Center) sold for $45,000. The x-ray was estimated to draw $1,200.

• The chair from her final photo shoot sold for $35,000.

• The Planet Hollywood Julien's Auction also included bank statements, signed checks and scripts.

NOTE: In April 2008 a federal court ruled that Marilyn Monroe was a New Yorker when she died. Her images under

California right of publicity law had earned her estate more than $30 million from licensing fees for the use of her images. Since Marilyn Monroe was determined to be a New Yorker at death, products may now use her image without paying licensing fees to the estate because of the differences between New York and California state laws.

This legal battle will surely continue for years to come.

Fast Facts:

Marilyn is reputed to have had an IQ score of 168 (100 is considered average and 150 is highly gifted).

Marilyn supposedly told photographer Bert Stern in 1962 that she always used Nivea Skin Moisturizing Lotion. It's surprising that Nivea didn't capitalize on this in their print and media ads.

In some publicity photos for *Some Like It Hot*, including the film's poster, a body double was used: Sandra Warren, an actress who appeared in the movie as one of Sweet Sue's Society Syncopators. Marilyn's face was superimposed over Sandra's body.

In March of 2008 the city of Glendale, California, announced an agreement to purchase Rockhaven Sanitarium, possibly for a library. Marilyn's mother, Billie Burke, and Francis Farmer were once residents.

Pets:

Marilyn Monroe Quote: "Dogs never bite me. Just humans," and "I like animals. If you talk to a dog or a cat, it doesn't tell you to shut up."

Tippy was a dog given to her by her foster father, Albert Wayne Bolender. Tippy was shot and killed by a neighbor who claimed that Tippy had been rolling around in his garden. Coincidentally, in her final, unfinished film, *Something's Got to Give*, the dog was named Tippy.

When she lived with the Goddard family, they had a pet spaniel.

Husband Jim Dougherty bought Muggsie, a collie, for Norma Jean.

She later owned a Chihuahua; a white Persian cat named Mitsou; a Basset Hound named Hugo; a parakeet called Butch; Ebony, a riding horse; and Maf, a white dog that was a gift from Frank Sinatra. Conflicting reports list Maf as a poodle and a Maltese. Following Marilyn's death, Maf was inherited by Frank Sinatra's secretary.

Favorites:

Favorite Clothing Designers: Pucci and Jax

Marilyn loved color. If she liked a particular dress, she'd have it in many colors. She had several Pucci long-sleeved as well as short-sleeved same style dresses in several colors. She was buried in a green Pucci dress.

Another favorite was Jax. She had four identically styled deep V-neck short dresses and used this dress as a prototype for the one she wore in 1960's *Let's Make Love*.

173

HELLO, NORMA JEAN

Tributes:

Young Hollywood seems to have a major love affair with Marilyn. Entertainers such as Scarlett Johannson (Scarlett looked to be channeling Marilyn in her Dolce & Gabbana print ads and in January of 2010, Scarlett made her Broadway debut in the revival of Arthur Miller's *A View From the Bridge*), Megan Fox (with Marilyn's face tattooed on her inner forearm), Mariah Carey, Charlize Theron, Nicole Kidman, Britney Spears, Heidi Montag and Paris Hilton have all expressed an admiration for Marilyn.

Lindsay Lohan: In 2008, 46 years after his 1962 photo shoot of Marilyn taken just 6-weeks before her death, called "The Last Sitting," noted photographer Bert Stern recreated these legendary photographs with Lindsay Lohan for the spring fashion issue of *New York* magazine. Lindsay also posed as Marilyn on the cover of the Spanish Vogue. In early 2007, she bought the 2-bedroom L. A. apartment where Marilyn once lived. Lindsay has two tattoos of quotes attributed to Marilyn: "Everyone's a star and deserves the right to twinkle" (a variation of which is also listed as a quote by Marilyn: "Everyone is a star and deserves a chance to shine") and "I restore myself when I'm alone."

Madonna: Madonna's 1985 "Material Girl" video captured the frothy beauty of Marilyn in the pink strapless gown from *Gentlemen Prefer Blondes*.

In the fall of 2009, Madonna's album, *Celebrations*, the third in her *Greatest Hits* collection, featured cover art that strongly suggests Andy Warhol's pop art Marilyn.

174

Anna Nicole Smith always expressed an interest in playing Marilyn Monroe in a film. It's reported that six months before her February 2007 death, Anna Nicole tried to finance a film based on Marv Schneider's book, *DiMaggio: Setting the Record Straight*, in which she would play Marilyn. She was turned down for the part.

Michelle Williams is slated to play Marilyn Monroe in *My Week With Marilyn*, based on the diary of Colin Clark, who looked after Marilyn when she came to London in 1957 to film *The Prince and the Showgirl* with Laurence Olivier. It is rumored that Kenneth Branagh will play Laurence Olivier, and Jake Jagger, the 25-year old son of Jerry Hall and Mick Jagger, may play Colin Clark in the film, to be directed by Simon Curtis. It is said that Ralph Fiennes was to have played Olivier but will instead direct *Coriolanus*.

My Week With Marilyn goes into production in September of 2010. Other actresses mentioned for consideration included Scarlett Johansson, Amy Adams and Kate Hudson.

Australian actress, Naomi Watts, will play Marilyn in the film *Blonde*, to be directed by Andrew Dominik. It is based on the Pulitzer Prize-nominated novel by Joyce Carol Oates, and set to start production in January of 2011.

In July of 2010, Angelina Jolie denied rumors that she is set to play Marilyn in the movie to be adapted from the novel, *The Life and Opinions of Maf the Dog, and of His Friend, Marilyn Monroe*, written by Andrew O'Hagan.

HELLO, NORMA JEAN

Songs:

"Candle in the Wind" written in 1973 to honor Marilyn Monroe. Music by Elton John and lyrics by Bernie Taupin.

> Goodbye Norma Jean
> Though I never knew you at all
> You had the grace to hold yourself
> While those around you crawled
> Goodbye Norma Jean
> From the young man in the 22nd row
> Who sees you as something more than sexual
> More than just our Marilyn Monroe

Joe Elliott of *Def Leppard* has said that their song, "Photograph," from their 1983 album *Pyromania*, was about Marilyn Monroe.

"Photograph," written by Joe Elliott, Pete Willis, Steve Clark, Rick Savage, and Robert John "Mutt" Lange:

> I see your face every time I dream
> on every page, every magazine
> So wild, so free, so far from me
> You're all I want, my fantasy

The Misfits, whose name was taken from Marilyn's final film, were formed in Lodi, New Jersey, in 1977.

"Who Killed Marilyn" written by Glenn Danzig

5:25 august fifth, 1962
found her lying on her chest
her face all turning blue
you think it was an overdose
but could it have been the pact
could it have been the Kennedys
was it L.A.P.D.
It ain't a mystery
baby, not to me

Personal Belongings:

As of July 2010 Debbie Reynolds owns the Marilyn
Monroe white dress from *Seven Year Itch* among her stellar
collection of Hollywood memorabilia. NOTE: To promote the
film *Seven Year Itch*, a 52-foot-high cutout of Marilyn in the
blowing dress scene was erected in front of New York's Loews
State Theater in Times Square, although this famous full-
length image of Marilyn was not even shown in the movie.
The shot in the film is only of her legs; the movie's poster with
Marilyn in the blowing dress made *Premiere*'s "25 Best Movie
Posters Ever."

Marilyn had always been an admirer of President
Abraham Lincoln. She was quoted as saying that she felt they
shared a similar childhood. She also reportedly said that Arthur
Miller reminded her of Lincoln.

In July 2007 a noted Marilyn Monroe memorabilia
collector donated one of Marilyn's dresses to the Lincoln
Presidential Library, possibly due to Marilyn's lifelong interest

in Lincoln and her friendship with Carl Sandburg, who
authored a well-respected biography of Lincoln.

On Exhibit:

Running June–August 2010 at the Hollywood Museum:
"Marilyn Remembered—An Intimate Look at the Legend."
Items from the Greg Schreiner Marilyn Monroe collection on
exhibit include Marilyn's personal travel trunk, Pucci blouse,
childhood book, and limo receipts. NOTE: Greg Schreiner is
the President and a founding member of Marilyn
Remembered, the respected, longest-running Marilyn fan club.

Actresses Who Have Portrayed Marilyn:

Naomi Watts in *My Week With Marilyn*, 2011
Michelle Williams in *Blonde*, 2011
Constance Forslund in *This Year's Blonde*, 1980
Catherine Hicks in *Marilyn, The Untold Story*, 1980
Theresa Russell as 'The Actress' in *Insignificance*, 1985
Heather Thomas in *Hoover vs. the Kennedys: The
Second Civil War*, 1987
Phoebe Legere in *Mondo New York*, 1988
Paula Lane in *Goodnight, Sweet Marilyn*, 1989
Arlene Lorre portrayed Marilyn in *Another Chance*,
1989
Susan Griffiths in *Pulp Fiction*, 1994
Sunshine H. Hernandez in *With Honors*, 1994
Jennifer Austin in *My Fellow Americans*, 1996
Ashley Judd as Norma Jean and Mira Sorvino as
Marilyn in *Norma Jean & Marilyn*, 1996

Nectar Rose (uncredited) in *L.A. Confidential*, 1997

Sunny Davis in *Jerry and Tom*, 1998

Sally Kirkland in *The Island*, 1998

Barbara Niven in *The Rat Pack*, 1998

Kim Little in *Evil Hill*, 1999

Kassandra Kay in *Red Lipstick*, 2000

Meredith Patterson in *Company Man*, 2000

Poppy Montgomery in *Blonde*, 2001

Holly Beavon (uncredited) in *James Dean*, 2001

Sophie Monk in *The Mystery of Natalie Wood*, 2004

Marilyn's Character Names:

Phone Operator (uncredited) in *The Shocking Miss Pilgrim*, 1947

Evie in *Dangerous Years*, 1947

Extra at square dance (uncredited) in *Green Grass of Wyoming*, 1948

Girl in canoe (uncredited) in *Scudda Hoo! Scudda Hay!*, 1948

Client in *Love Happy*, 1949

Peggy in *Ladies of the Chorus*, 1949

Dusky (uncredited) in *Right Cross*, 1950

Angela in *The Asphalt Jungle*, 1950

Clara (uncredited) in *A Ticket to Tomahawk*, 1950

Miss Casswell in *All About Eve*, 1950

Polly in *The Fireball*, 1950

Joyce in *Let's Make It Legal*, 1951

Bobbie in *Love Nest*, 1951

Harriet in *As Young as You Feel*, 1951

Iris in *Home Town Story*, 1951

Lois in *Monkey Business*, 1952
Streetwalker in *O. Henry's Full House*, 1952
Nell in *Don't Bother to Knock*, 1952
Annabel in *We're Not Married!*, 1952
Peggy in *Clash by Night*, 1952
Pola in *How to Marry a Millionaire*, 1953
Lorelei Lee in *Gentlemen Prefer Blondes*, 1953
NOTE: Judy Holliday turned down this role because she
felt that Carol Channing, who played Lorelei Lee on
Broadway, should play the role.
Rose in *Niagara*, 1953
Vicky in *There's No Business Like Show Business*, 1954
Kay in *River of No Return*, 1954
The Girl in *The Seven Year Itch*, 1955
Cherie in *Bus Stop*, 1956
Elsie in *The Prince and the Showgirl*, 1957
Sugar Kane in *Some Like It Hot*, 1959
NOTE: It has been rumored that it took more than 40
takes for Marilyn to master the one line, "Where's that
bourbon?"
Amanda in *Let's Make Love*, 1960
Roslyn in *The Misfits*, 1961
Ellen in *Something's Got to Give*, 1962

Marilyn's Songs in her Films:

"I'm Through With Love" in *Some Like It Hot*, 1959
"Heat Wave" in *There's No Business Like Show
Business*, 1954
"A Little Girl from Little Rock" with Jane Russell in
Gentlemen Prefer Blondes, 1953

"Bye Bye Baby" in *Gentlemen Prefer Blondes*, 1953

"Diamonds are a Girl's Best Friend" in *Gentlemen Prefer Blondes*, 1953

"Kiss" in *Niagara*, 1953

"I'm Gonna File My Claim" in *River of No Return*, 1954

"River of No Return," title song from the film, 1954

NOTE: Before "Candle in the Wind" there was a song about Marilyn, called "Marilyn," written for Ray Anthony by Jimmy Shirl and Ervin M. Drake:

> An angel in lace, a fabulous face
> That's no exaggeration, that's my Marilyn
> No gal, I believe,
> Beginning with Eve
> Could weave a fascination like my Marilyn

Interview Excerpts:

LIFE magazine:

Excerpts from 8-hours of tape that resulted in Marilyn's last interview published by *LIFE* magazine on August 3, 1962, two days before her death. The subject was fame:

"I'm not calling myself an orphan but I was brought up a waif."

"If I am a star, the people made me a star."

"Sometimes people want to see if you're real."

"Some of my foster families used to send me to the movies to get me out of the house and there I'd sit all day and way into the night."

"Sexuality is only attractive when it's natural and spontaneous."

"I was never used to being happy, so that wasn't something I ever took for granted."

NOTE: Excerpts from the audiotape of the interview were combined with images and film clips of Marilyn into a 30-minute special shown on HBO on July 20, 1992. This TV special can be viewed in two parts online by going to YouTube and searching for "Marilyn Monroe The Last Interview."

Person to Person:

From Edward R. Murrow's interview on *Person to Person* that aired April 8, 1955. During a discussion about being captured in a picture as she rode a pink elephant (at a charity event in Madison Square Garden):

"I think it meant a lot because, probably because I hadn't been to a circus as a kid."

Portions of this interview can be viewed online by going to YouTube and searching for "Marilyn Monroe Person to Person Interview."

Time Yahoo Chat: In the late Dominick Dunne's December 1999 *Time* Yahoo Chat about the release of his book, *The Way We Lived Then*, Dominick said that he was under contract at Twentieth Century Fox, and Marilyn was much loved on the lot (but not by the executives because of her many takes). He also believed that Marilyn had been involved with both Robert and John F. Kennedy. Here's the link:

http://www.time.com/time/community/transcripts/1999/121399dunne.html

CNN's Larry King Live: Quotes from the June 1, 2001, airing of CNN's *Larry King Live: Remembering Marilyn Monroe.* Guests included the following:

Tony Curtis, who starred with Marilyn in *Some Like it Hot.* NOTE: In October 2009, with the release of his book, *The Making of Some Like it Hot,* Curtis dropped the bombshell that Marilyn had become pregnant by him and miscarried while she was married to Arthur Miller.

Jane Russell, Marilyn's co-star in *Gentlemen Prefer Blondes.*

Donald O'Connor, who was in *There's No Business Like Show Business* with Marilyn.

Famed photojournalist George Barris, who did Marilyn's final photo shoot.

Former *LIFE* magazine editor Richard Meryman, who interviewed Marilyn at length just a few weeks before her death.

Renowned movie producer David Brown, the original producer of Marilyn's last film, *Something's Got to Give.*

James Haspiel, Marilyn's friend and author of *The Unpublished Marilyn.*

RICHARD MERYMAN: I felt that she was terribly vulnerable, terribly needy, terribly distrustful. She felt betrayed right and left.

DONALD O'CONNOR; Always found her to be a lot of fun, a lot of joy.

TONY CURTIS: She was the best. Marilyn was not that complicated, guys. She wasn't that vulnerable, either. She was a tough, beautiful woman.

NOTE: During the show Tony Curtis admits that the quote attributed to him, that "kissing Marilyn was like kissing Hitler," was meant as a joke in response to an inane question, "What's it like kissing Marilyn Monroe." This was said after years of his denying ever having made the legendary statement.

JANE RUSSELL: Well, when I worked with Marilyn it was really only her second starring role and she was shy about going out on the set.

BARRIS: She was a delight. I don't know what anyone else says about her, but we hit it off great.

DAVID BROWN: She was a brilliant woman. She had a great sense of story. She wanted to be a fine actress.

JAMES HASPIEL: I knew a very productive woman who was very, very busy in her life, taking her acting lessons and doing the kinds of things that made her invention, meaning Marilyn Monroe, an even better presentation to her prospective audience.

BARRIS: She had nobody. Who did she go home to? No family, no children.

The full transcript of the show is at http://transcripts.cnn.com/TRANSCRIPTS/0106/01/lkl.00.html.

CNN's Larry King Live: Quotes from the August 21, 2005 airing of CNN's *Larry King Live: Encore Presentation: Panel Discusses Marilyn Monroe.* Guests included:

Noted actress Jane Russell: "She was dear, and she was smart. She was very shy."

Author, journalist, Hollywood columnist and close friend of Marilyn's, James Bacon: "She was very sweet and very vulnerable, you know, and very charming, witty. God, she was a great gal."

Elegant actress and Marilyn's friend, Arlene Dahl (who introduced Marilyn to Jack Kennedy): "Marilyn was very sweet, very misunderstood, very vulnerable."

"I think that Marilyn was a girl with ambition but she was looking for love, she wanted to be loved more than anything."

The full transcript of the show is at http://transcripts.cnn.com/TRANSCRIPTS/0508/21/lkl.01.html

Additional Notes:

At 19, Berniece Baker learned of her 12-year old half-sister, Marilyn, when she received a letter from their mother, Gladys. Marilyn's half-brother, Robert Kermit Baker, called "Jack" or "Jackie," had died in 1932. After exchanging letters for several years, the half-sisters finally met in 1944.

Marilyn attended nine different schools and took a few evening literature and art appreciation classes at UCLA.

Marilyn lived at 45+ addresses.

Marilyn owned only one home. After her marriage to Arthur Miller broke up, she returned to Los Angeles and bought her first and only home, 12305 5th Helena Drive in Brentwood, California. She bought the modest home in February of 1962 for $77,500 (as of August 2010, the house is currently on the market for $3.5 million). The one-story, two bedroom, L-shaped Spanish colonial home had adobe walls, a red-tiled roof, a small guesthouse, a swimming pool, and a garden. The interior had white stucco walls, white carpeting, beamed ceilings and tiled fireplaces in the living room and master bedroom. Monroe bought a few furnishings in Mexico, but the house remained sparsely furnished.

At the age of seven months she'd been baptized by the renowned Pentecostal evangelist Aimee Semple McPherson (Sister Aimee) in her Angelus Temple of the International Church, located in the Echo Park district of Los Angeles.

Marilyn reportedly had affairs with Milton Berle, Orson Welles, columnist Jim Bacon, Elia Kazan, Howard Hughes and Marlon Brando.

It is said that Marilyn turned down the lead female role in 1958's *Some Came Running*. Ultimately played by Shirley MacLaine, this role earned Shirley a Best Actress Academy Award nomination. Marilyn also turned down the lead in *Can-Can*.

Lee Strasberg reportedly said that the two greatest acting

talents he worked with were Marlon Brando and Marilyn Monroe. This is quite an honor, considering that the following actors studied with him at the Actor's Studio: Robert DeNiro, Al Pacino, Paul Newman, Montgomery Clift, James Dean, Eli Wallach, Jane Fonda, Maureen Stapleton, and Steve McQueen.

Marilyn attended classes in New York with Constance Collier and with Lee Strasberg. Marilyn was not a member of Strasberg's renowned Actor's Studio. She was reportedly planning to join The Actor's Studio in the fall of 1962.

Last lines in the movie, *The Misfits*, delivered by Marilyn Monroe and Clark Gable, both of whom would soon die:

ROSLYN (Monroe): How do you find your way back in the dark?
GAY (Gable): Just head for that big star straight on. The highway's under it. It'll take us right home.

Allegedly, Truman Capote wanted Marilyn to play his beloved Holly Golightly character in the screen adaptation of his stellar novella, *Breakfast at Tiffany's*. She was also said to be playwright Tennessee Williams' first choice to play the childish bride in Elia Kazan's film version of *Baby Doll*.

In October of 2008, Marilyn earned the dubious honor of yet again making *Forbes* magazine's list of the thirteen Top Earning Dead Celebrities, joining Elvis and James Dean. She had been on the list eight years running since it debuted in 2001. Marilyn did not make the list released in October 2009 due to the $350 million estate sale revenue for designer Yves Saint Laurent (number one on the 2009 listing) and the death of Michael Jackson, whose estate brought in $90 million.

Marilyn as Roslyn in *The Misfits* closes a closet door that has pin-up photos of Marilyn Monroe.

In *The Seven Year Itch*, Richard Sherman played by Tom Ewell is talking with the janitor, Mr. Kruhulik, played by Robert Strauss, about Richard having a blonde in the kitchen. Richard says, "Maybe it's Marilyn Monroe."

In film versions of William Somerset Maugham's *Sadie Thompson*, legendary actresses had played the lead role: Gloria Swanson in 1927's *Sadie Thompson*, Joan Crawford in 1931's *Rain*, and Rita Hayworth in the 1946 version of *Sadie Thompson*. Marilyn hoped to prove herself a serious actress in a television version with her Sadie Thompson being directed by Lee Strasberg. Supposedly the deal was never made because NBC insisted on a director with TV experience.

When Marilyn was in Canada filming *River of No Return* with Robert Mitchum,* formidable director Otto Preminger actually banned Marilyn's acting coach, Natasha Lytess, from the set. It was reported that Marilyn was relying on Natasha to 'direct' her scenes rather than Preminger. The location shooting was also fraught with accidents: Marilyn and Mitchum's raft got stuck on rocks and was dangerously close to turning over when two stuntmen rescued them by lifeboat, and later in the filming Marilyn injured her ankle and required a plaster cast.

*Coincidentally Robert Mitchum worked at an airplane factory with Marilyn's first husband, Jimmy Dougherty.

Noted Marilyn Monroe collector Mark Bellinghaus, who for years has championed for the authenticity of all Marilyn Monroe memorabilia, questioned the validity of items featured in the 2005 Marilyn Monroe Exhibit aboard the Queen Mary, in particular a set of Clairol Hair Rollers said to contain the real hair of Marilyn Monroe. These rollers were manufactured in 1974, 12 years after her death. He filed a class action lawsuit against the Queen Mary (settled out of court in April of 2007). Mark Bellinghaus shared his stellar collection in June 2006 at the Hollywood Museum.

Ghost Stories:

The supposed image of Marilyn Monroe in the Hollywood Roosevelt Hotel's mirror: It has long been rumored that the Hollywood Roosevelt Hotel is haunted by Marilyn (and by Montgomery Clift). The famous hotel, financed by Mary Pickford and her swashbuckling husband, Douglas Fairbanks, Jr., was host to the first Academy Awards ceremony in May of 1929.

Marilyn stayed at the hotel and the full-length mirror from her poolside suite was moved to the manager's office. It was in this office that an employee saw the distinct face of Marilyn Monroe. The mirror was moved to the hotel's lobby by the elevators for all guests to hopefully catch a glance of the hotel's famous patron. In early 2006, singer Nick Lachey allegedly saw Marilyn's image as he entered the hotel's elevator.

Coincidentally, story is that Marilyn posed for her very first ad, for a suntan lotion, on the Hollywood Roosevelt's swimming pool diving board.

NOTE: In later years Marilyn often used the pseudonym Zelda Zonk when checking into hotels.

Reportedly, her image has also been seen in her cabin at Lake Tahoe's Cal Neva Resort, formerly owned by Frank Sinatra.

Marilyn in Cabin #3, Lake Tahoe's Cal Neva Resort, Spa and Casino:

Cal Neva, a huge lodge on the California/Nevada state line, was built in 1926. There is a room that has a painted line showing the California and Nevada split.

Lake Tahoe's Cal Neva, nicknamed "The Lady of the Lake," was bought by Frank Sinatra in the mid-fifties. He had tunnels added under the property to provide an escape from paparazzi for his frequent guest celebrities, including Marilyn Monroe, Kennedy family members, Sam Giancana of the Chicago Mafia, Judy Garland, Dean Martin, Sammy Davis, Jr, and Juliet Prowse.

Days before her death, Marilyn stayed in Cabin #3, her favorite. The cabin still stands but as of June 2009 the Cal Neva is facing foreclosure. Many guests have reported seeing the ghost of Marilyn in Cabin #3.

Since Giancana had been banned from Nevada casinos, his visit to Cal Neva in July of 1963 and subsequent fight with the manager of his girlfriend, Phyllis McGuire of the McGuire Sisters, brought unwanted attention to the resort. In early October of 1963, Sinatra exited the property and its ownership.

Photos:

It's hard to believe that there are actually any unpublished photos of Marilyn still available, but in February 2010 LIFE.com published Loomis Dean's photographs of Marilyn from 1952. These unpublished photos of a then 25-year old Marilyn Monroe were taken at a party thrown by the Foreign Press Association of Hollywood (an event now known as the "*Golden Globe(s)*®"), where Marilyn had just won the "Henrietta Award" for Best Young Box Office Personality.

Within months of these photos, Marilyn would appear on her first cover of *LIFE* magazine.

In February of 2010, Len Steckler released his never-before-seen photographs of Marilyn visiting Pulitzer prize winning poet Carl Sandburg in 1961.

Videos:

Despite rumors of a "stag" film short supposedly starring a young Marilyn, it was actually Arline Hunter, *Playboy*'s Playmate of the Month for August 1954, a Marilyn look-alike.

NOTE: Marilyn won a court case in 1952 that she brought against men who were promoting a "stag" film in which she supposedly starred.

In April of 2008, a memorabilia collector claimed to have discovered a silent 15-minute black-and-white pornographic video of Marilyn from the 1950s. He stated that Joe DiMaggio allegedly offered to pay $25,000 for the film to keep it from the public, but the offer was refused. Since the buyer who supposedly paid $1.5 million keeps the film locked away, it has not been determined if this film is legitimate or a hoax.

In late 2009 a video surfaced that allegedly shows Marilyn smoking pot.

Quotes From Others About Marilyn:

"Marilyn was an incredible person to act with...the most marvelous I ever worked with, and I have been working for 29 years."

> *Montgomery Clift*
> *Academy Award winning actor*
> *who played Perce in The Misfits*

"I got a cold chill...She got sex on a piece of film like Jean Harlow."

> *Leon Shamroy*
> *4-time Academy Award winning*
> *cinematographer, regarding Marilyn's 1946 screen test*

"She looked like if you bit her, milk and honey would flow from her."

> *Franz Kline*
> *American artist*

"She was not the usual movie idol. She was the type who would join in and wash up the supper dishes even if you didn't ask her."

> *Carl Sandburg*
> *legendary poet who, according to some,*
> *was in love with Marilyn*

"Marilyn was so bright about acting. Her trouble was only that she'd get so scared she wasn't going to be able to do it, and so tied up in knots that everyone thought she was dumb."

Peggy Feury
actress and respected drama teacher

"Marilyn's need to be desired was so great that she could make love to a camera."

William Manchester
historian and biographer
who wrote 18 books, including
two about John Kennedy

"The trouble with Marilyn was she didn't trust her own judgment."

Allan 'Whitey' Snyder
Emmy-nominated leading Hollywood make-up artist
and Marilyn's personal make-up artist

"Hollywood, Broadway, the night clubs all produce their quota of sex queens but the public takes them or leaves them; the world is not as enslaved by them as it was by Marilyn Monroe because none but she could suggest such a purity of sexual delight."

Diana Trilling
literary critic and author

"She'd come out of our apartment in a shleppy old coat, looking like my maid, and all the people would push her aside to get my autograph. She loved it."

Shelley Winters
Academy Award winning actress and author

"Miss Marilyn Monroe calls to mind the bouquet of a fireworks display."

Sir Cecil Beaton
British fashion and portrait photographer
and Academy Award winning stage
and film costume designer

"I had always thought that all those amusing remarks she was supposed to have made for the press had probably been manufactured and mimeographed by her press agent, but they weren't. She was a very bright person, an instinctive type."

Elliott Erwitt
noted photographer

"On the surface, she was still a happy girl. But those who criticized her never saw her as I did, crying like a baby because she often felt herself so inadequate."

Travilla
Academy Award and Emmy winning costume designer
who worked with Marilyn on eight of her movies

"You say hello to her or it's a nice day today, and she answers with a line from the script. She forgets everything but the work."

Jean Negulesco
director and screenwriter

"She had such magnetism that if 15 men were in a room with her, each man would be convinced he was the one she'd be waiting for after the others left."

Roy Craft
publicist with Twentieth Century Fox

"Dietrich made sex remote, Garbo made it mysterious, Crawford made it agonizing, but Monroe makes it amusing. Whenever a man thinks of Marilyn, he smiles at his own thoughts."

Milton Shulman
film and theatre critic and author

"She knows the world, but this knowledge has not lowered her great and benevolent dignity, its darkness has not dimmed her goodness."

Edith Sitwell
poetess

"She is a beautiful child. I don't think she's an actress at all, not in a traditional sense. What she has—this presence, this luminosity, this flickering intelligence—could never surface on the stage. It's so fragile and subtle, it can only be caught by the camera."

Constance Collier
actress and acting coach

"She's the type of actor who you couldn't take your eyes off walking to, or away from you."

Groucho Marx
entertainer

Commentary by Ayn Rand, noted author of *Atlas Shrugged* and *The Fountainhead*, excerpted from *The Voice of Reason*, originally published two weeks after the death of Marilyn Monroe:

The death of Marilyn Monroe shocked people with an impact different from their reaction to the death

of any other movie star or public figure. All over
the world, people felt a peculiar sense of personal
involvement and of protest, like a universal cry of
"Oh, no!"
If there ever was a victim of society, Marilyn
Monroe was that victim—of a society that
professes dedication to the relief of the suffering,
but kills the joyous.

Quotes from Marilyn:

The lonely: *"A career is wonderful, but you can't curl up
with it on a cold night."*

The vulnerable: *"A sex symbol becomes a thing. I just
hate to be a thing."*

The bitter: *"An actress is not a machine but they treat
you like a machine. A money machine."*

The defeated: *"Being a sex symbol is a heavy load to
carry, especially when one is tired, hurt and bewildered."*

The cynical: *"Hollywood is a place where they'll pay you
a thousand dollars for a kiss and fifty cents for your soul."*

The poignant: *"It's all make believe, isn't it?"*

And the ironic—in Marilyn's own words, *"Sometimes I
think it would be easier to avoid old age, to die young but then
you'd never complete your life, would you? You'd never wholly
know yourself..."*

SUE DOLLERIS

HELLO, NORMA JEAN

About the Author

Constantly inspired, I welcome inspiration and am practically handed the manuscript, screenplay, or short story in its entirety. I can barely type fast enough to capture their stories. Over the years, I've learned to fine tune the nuances of inspiration into feasible works. Born and raised in Louisville, Kentucky, I'm a writer who masquerades as a Medical Recruiter during the day. I am married with two grown daughters and have lived in Nashville, Tennessee for more than twenty years.
Author website at http://normajean.yolasite.com/

HELLO, NORMA JEAN

If you enjoyed *Hello, Norma Jean*, consider these other fine books from Savant Books and Publications:

A Whale's Tale by Daniel S. Janik
Tropic of California by R. Page Kaufman
The Village Curtain by Tony Tame
Dare to Love in Oz by William Maltese
The Interzone by Tasuyuki Kobayashi
Today I Am A Man by Larry Rodness
The Bahrain Conspiracy by Bentley Gates
Called Home by Gloria Schumann
Kanaka Blues by Mike Farris
First Breath edited by Zachary M. . Oliver
Poor Rich by Jean Blasiar
The Jumper Chronicles by W. C. Peever
William Maltese's Flicker by William Maltese
My Unborn Child by Orest Stocco
Last Song of the Whales by Four Arrows
Perilous Panacea by Ronald Klueh
Falling but Fulfilled by Zachary M. Oliver
Still Life with Cat and Mouse by Sheila McGraw
Mythical Voyage by Robin Ymer
Manifest Intent by Mike Farris

Soon to be Released:
Ammon's Horn by Guerrino Amati
In the Himalayan Nights by Anoop Chandola
In Dire Straits by Jim Curry
Charlie No Face by David Seaburn
Richer by Jean Blasiar
Number One Bestseller by Brian Morley
Blood Money by Scott Mastro
The Treasure of La Econdida by Carolyn Kingson
Wretched Land by Mila Komarnisky
My Two Wives and Three Husbands by S. Stanley Gordon

http://www.savantbooksandpublications.com